Brisa was prepared to smile, wave and slowly fade away.

Watching father and daughter caused that weird ache in the center of Brisa's chest to return.

Thea stood and wrapped her arms around Brisa's waist before squeezing. "You didn't have to take me to see the stars. I really appreciate it."

Brisa had to clear her throat before she could answer. "I enjoyed every minute, Thea."

When she stepped back, Thea tilted her head to the side. "Think about what I said. About my dad." She waggled her eyebrows before picking up her bag. "I'm going to pack my stuff for tonight, Dad. Daylight's wasting."

She disappeared into her room before Wade turned back to Brisa. "Are you exhausted?" he asked. "I'm sure she'd be happy to arrange more sculling practice if you'd like."

If Brisa didn't get away from the McNallys soon, she was going to make a fool of herself. Apart, they were great; together, they were devastating to her emotions.

Dear Reader,

I've enjoyed writing sisters. Do you have a sister? I don't, but my two older brothers are smart and much cooler than I've ever been.

My heroine, Brisa Montero, is the youngest in the family, just like me. Catfishing surgeon Wade McNally on behalf of her older sister, the Montero family's superstar, is a small mess that Brisa has to clean up before anyone else finds out.

Wade has his own knot to untangle—a daughter he loves but doesn't know. They'll learn that life can be messy and confusing and so sweet when they're figuring it out together.

To find out more about my books and what's coming next, visit me at cherylharperbooks.com.

Cheryl

HEARTWARMING

The Doctor and the Matchmaker

———

Cheryl Harper

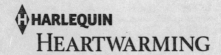

HARLEQUIN
HEARTWARMING

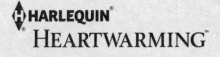

® HARLEQUIN®
HEARTWARMING™

Recycling programs
for this product may
not exist in your area.

ISBN-13: 978-1-335-17979-1

The Doctor and the Matchmaker

Copyright © 2021 by Cheryl Harper

This edition published by arrangement with Harlequin Books S.A.

For questions and comments about the quality of this book,
please contact us at CustomerService@Harlequin.com.

Harlequin Enterprises ULC
22 Adelaide St. West, 40th Floor
Toronto, Ontario M5H 4E3, Canada
www.Harlequin.com

Printed in U.S.A.

Cheryl Harper discovered her love for books and words as a little girl, thanks to a mother who made countless library trips, and an introduction to Laura Ingalls Wilder's Little House books. Whether the stories she reads are set in the prairie, the American West, Regency England or Earth a hundred years in the future, Cheryl enjoys strong characters who make her laugh. Now Cheryl spends her days searching for the right words while she stares out the window and her dog, Jack, snoozes beside her. And she considers herself very lucky to do so.

For more information about Cheryl's books, visit her online at cherylharperbooks.com or follow her on Twitter, @cherylharperbks.

Books by Cheryl Harper

Harlequin Heartwarming

Veterans' Road

The Dalmatian Dilemma
A Soldier Saved

Otter Lake Ranger Station

Her Unexpected Hero
Her Heart's Bargain
Saving the Single Dad
Smoky Mountain Sweethearts

Visit the Author Profile page
at Harlequin.com for more titles.

For my big brothers, thank you.

CHAPTER ONE

BRISA MONTERO LOVED the spotlight. Other people were at home in boardrooms or operating rooms or airplane cockpits, but Brisa understood what was expected of her when she was center stage.

Stages themselves weren't even necessary; only the audience mattered. The most exclusive hotel on Miami's South Beach had built a small stage for her father's rooftop cocktail party. Brisa had been a nervous wreck to step up on it this time, but she'd done it.

She and her sister, Reyna, had managed to win a significant battle of wills on the stage that efficient hotel staff were now dismantling.

Brisa was going to have a chance to run Concord Court, the townhome complex her father had built to house veterans leaving military service while they pursued new careers or educational opportunities. Luis Montero had intended to lure Reyna home with Concord Court, a safe way to continue serving and add some luster to the family name at the same time. Instead, Reyna made her own way as she always had, and Brisa had stepped up. No one expected Brisa to do as well as Reyna, but the job was hers.

More important than the job was the shot at proving herself to her family. Another shot.

After years of failures.

This could be her last shot.

Making firm fists kept her hands from trembling. Brisa knew how to convince others that she was fine. A sparkling smile. The graceful touch of a shoulder as she worked the crowd. Always nodding at the right spot in the conversation.

That was her version of automatic pilot to guarantee the smooth operation of one of her father's philanthropic events.

But the size of the job she'd fought to get and the high stakes were sinking in.

"You ready to go, babe?" Reggie Beaumont asked, one hand on the door that led from the hotel's rooftop to the small cocktail bar and the elevators beyond. In the other hand? His trusty cell phone. Apparently, he'd finished making the phone calls that had kept him busy all night long. He'd missed her big victory completely. "The car's downstairs waiting. I'll drop you off wherever you need to go." He was tall and handsome in a perfectly tailored suit that fit her father's tastes to a T, even if a professional athlete would never have been Luis Montero's idea of a suitable partner for one of his daughters.

That fact was Reggie's best feature.

Brisa straightened her shoulders. Earlier in the evening, she'd wanted a confidence boost from him, but he'd been occupied talking to his agent. His contract negotiations were making headlines.

Most of the time, Reggie's lack of attention didn't bother Brisa at all. Reggie's number one job was to keep her father's matchmaking attempts at bay. For that, he was perfect. They had the best understanding; nothing was serious between them. No emotional ties were expected.

Tonight was the first time she wished for

the support of someone who cared for her as more than an acquaintance who opened the right doors and posed beautifully in press photos.

But the night was over. She didn't need him anymore.

"I've got to stay behind, make sure everything is taken care of. You go ahead." Brisa ran a hand down his lapel. "Thanks for watching my back again, handsome."

Mindful of the small audience that might still be watching them, Reggie held her for a minute before kissing her cheek. "Anytime, beautiful, especially if the club is catering. Can't get enough of their shrimp." Then he held up a hand and stepped inside without hesitating. Why would he? All the people that mattered had left. Even the hotel staff was dwindling. The musicians had been the first to go. The caterers were wrapping up.

"Your sister has gone already," her father said as he stopped in front of her. "Not that we enjoyed much of her and Wakefield's attention after your announcement. They managed to find an invisible corner for…conversation." Luis Montero cleared his throat. Brisa would bet every dollar her father had that Reyna and Sean Wakefield had been doing more kissing than talking; her father was no dummy, either. Brisa had missed their courtship, but it was impossible to miss the way they stared at each other now. "I should not have been ambushed by you and your sister like this, Brisa. Do not suppose I have let it go. It was an underhanded maneuver, switching jobs like that. It might occasionally be appropriate in business, but where is the place for that in this family?" He tugged his suit coat to eliminate any wrinkle that had the audacity to appear.

Brisa bit back her immediate argument and exchanged a glance with Marisol. Her stepmother had been her biggest ally all these years Reyna had been stationed elsewhere with the Air Force. Ironing out a relationship with her father's third wife had taken some time, but Marisol had proven to be an ally in negotiations with Brisa's father. Brisa's mother sometimes remembered to send cards on birthdays, and her first stepmother was friendly enough now that Brisa and her sister were adults, but Marisol had stayed. Even faced with a teenage Brisa, she'd stayed. They were so close now, they could communicate without speaking. Her stepmom's expression said, *Be careful, but be strong.*

It was good advice. Slipping back into her normal pattern with her father was easy, even if it didn't fit perfectly. She loved him. He loved her. There was never any doubt about that.

Brisa squeezed her father's hand. "Daddy, we tried using logic. You know that's always Reyna's first choice. When that failed, Montero stubbornness kicked in. Reyna deserves to live her dream. She wants to be a firefighter." Her older sister had already been a decorated military officer and pilot so it made perfect sense she would need a big second career. Brisa wasn't going to spend any more time resenting that. She was so happy to have Reyna home full-time that falling under her shadow again wasn't an issue. "Just like I deserve a chance to run Concord Court. I can do this." She was almost sure she could. With Reyna's support and Sean Wakefield in his spot, taking care of the operations at the Court, and some luck, she *could* do this.

"Of course, you deserve this. You've been involved from the beginning, working at your father's side," Marisol agreed softly. "Your concept for the small business lab to support veteran-owned businesses? Genius. And nobody else came up with it." Not Reyna. Not Luis Montero. Marisol didn't add the last part, but the way her father frowned at his wife convinced Brisa he'd read between the lines.

"No more sneaking around. The two of you together…" He sighed. "I should have expected this, I suppose. You were always troublesome when you were together. The summer you plotted to build a tree house using the remnants of the old garden toolshed is hard to forget."

"We never meant to make the gardener cry." They'd wanted a place to paint and play and build and be free of the heavy weight of the Montero house's expectations. Her father had always preferred furniture and architecture that carried the importance and richness of history. His second wife had even kept an interior designer on retainer for decor emergencies. Brisa and Reyna had been good at creating those emergencies.

"I'll tell my gardener that when I meet with him next. I'm sure it will be a comfort to him, after all this time, that scaring him out of ten years of his life by falling out of the tree was only an accident, not an intentional decision." Her father didn't smile. He didn't make jokes. Never had.

Brisa clamped her hand over her left wrist. Covering up the scar there from where she'd broken it during that fall was a nervous habit.

That scar was no one's fault but her own. She'd begged Reyna to help her convince their father they needed a tree house. After he'd said no, Reyna had been determined they would do it on their own. Neither she nor her sister had understood the weakness of rotten wood at that point.

"I'll be watching your work at Concord Court closely, daughter." Her father dipped his chin and crooked his elbow. Marisol hugged Brisa before she slipped her hand through the bend in his arm. Their eyes met again and the quirk to her stepmother's lips was sweet. Openly mocking her father was a step too far, but being amused by him was part of Brisa's bond to Marisol.

"I'll need your help, Daddy. You know that. I know it, too." Brisa tipped her chin up. "But this is going to work." It had to. The fact that she'd been working so hard to learn the ropes and even expand the programs offered at Concord Court should have been evidence of her capability. However, reminding her father that they'd been sneaking around under his nose that way was a terrible idea.

"I want it to, Brisa. This must be a new chapter for the Monteros." He studied her face before nodding. "We'll talk this week. Expect me on Monday."

Marisol winked and they disappeared inside the cocktail bar.

Brisa braced her arms on the rooftop's wall. "Great job, Brisa. You plan parties better than anyone I know. String music at sunset with a view of the ocean was a nice change from the club. You've done it again. Everything went off without a hitch, even though I don't pay you to do this." Brisa threw her arms out. "In fact, I don't even ask you to do this anymore. I just assume you owe me your unpaid labor."

Because I pay all your bills.

Brisa's shoulders slumped as she realized that being irritated at her father's treatment of her and expectations was weakened spectacularly because the unspoken part had been true for too long.

"Is this a conversation anyone can join?" a man asked from behind her. Brisa took a minute to set her smile in place. Being rude to one of her father's friends wouldn't help her case at this point. This wasn't the first time one of them had hung around to introduce himself. Politely brushing off dinner invitations had grown much easier over the years.

As she turned, their eyes locked and it took longer than Brisa liked to realize who he was. He had on a nice but unremarkable suit with a dark tie and a plain watch. In this crowd, clothes shouted money. His said he worked hard for a living that didn't include custom suits.

This wasn't the first time she'd noticed him that evening, but it had always been a split second before the nerves over her announcement that she was stepping up to lead at Concord Court had washed over her and she would lose sight of him in the crowd.

That itch in her brain that convinced her she knew him, but couldn't recall his name returned.

Then she realized who he was.

The suit had confused her. His hard stare had thrown her off. In his Military Match profile, Wade McNally had worn the Navy's khaki service uniform. She remembered dark hair with touches of silver at the temples. Dark eyes. Impressive career as a Navy surgeon. Firm jaw and the implacable expression her sister sometimes used to put people in their place. He was the man she'd chosen for Reyna, the future date who would act as Reggie did, and thwart their father's matchmaking attempts to form dynastic unions with other well-meaning corporate elites.

But what was he doing here?

Brisa had ended everything with Wade McNally as soon as her sister had kissed Sean Wakefield in a dark corner of the pool area at Concord Court, in full view of the informal group that had gathered there. Brisa had confessed to Wade via text that she'd been running the Military Match ad for her sister, who had no idea she was doing so, and then quickly removed the profile she'd built for Reyna.

That should have worked. Ghosting. Wasn't that what they called it when a match disappeared? Brisa had never tried a dating app; Wade McNally probably wasn't an expert, either.

But here he was.

"Don't let me interrupt." Wade braced a shoulder against the doors, cutting off her only graceful exit. "I can wait until you finish talking to yourself to ask my questions."

Hmm. Her best defense had always been evasion. Could she still get out of this?

"Have we met?" Brisa tried as she watched the last of the hotel workers push two carts between them. Wade held the door open for them.

Then they were alone.

"Have we been introduced? Not officially, no. You're wondering why I'm here, *how* I'm here tonight. Your father invited me." Wade moved away from the door. She could escape if she wanted to, but he was studying her closely. "I met Luis at a hospital board meeting this week. I'm starting a new job as a trauma surgeon and the chief of staff wanted to introduce me."

At one point, she'd asked if he was ready to meet Reyna, before the kiss at the pool, and he'd explained he was in the process of moving to Miami. Apparently, that move was finished.

"Trauma surgeon. You're kind of a big deal. That's my father's favorite type of introduction," Brisa said and then cleared her throat when he didn't politely chuckle.

Wade put one hand in his pocket. Nothing about him suggested he was amused by their conversation. "Luis was full of pride about Concord Court and this party he was throwing to introduce his daughter, Reyna, the Air Force veteran, to his clients and friends. He wanted to brag about all the good work she was doing there, the programs, the number of veterans they'd be able to serve in a new way.

"Since I'd only heard of one other Reyna, an Air Force pilot also living in Miami, one who was being used in a strange catfishing scheme through Military Match, the dating app I joined a month ago…" Wade straightened his tie. "When he invited me, I came. I couldn't miss a chance to meet the one woman I've been interested in on the cursed dating app, even if she had never been real in the first place because her sister was playing matchmaker without permission."

As Brisa considered what she might say in response to his cold, harsh words, she realized how tired she was. In that minute, everything hurt. She'd been working full days at Concord Court and handling all the last-minute details of completing a bloodless takeover under her father's nose and throwing a Montero-level party. She stepped out of her heels and immediately felt better.

"Why am I not shocked his second daughter didn't make the sales pitch to the important new trauma surgeon," Brisa muttered to herself before she tilted her chin up. "I'm sorry. I never should have involved you in our family drama. I was trying to help my sister because I still haven't learned that I make a mess of things that Reyna never would. I didn't learn it at twenty or thirty. At this point, I might be a lost cause." She shook a finger at him. "Mister Navy Surgeon being recruited by hospitals all over the United States after years of dedicated service to your country. You might have a hot mess sibling, too. It happens that way. One who can do no wrong, and then the other child." Charm. It had always worked.

Wade shook his head. "Only child. Grew up in foster care. Can't relate."

Brisa had no answer for that. The tension between them grew heavy.

"At least you aren't trying to pretend you don't know who I am." *Anymore.* Wade didn't add that last part. Brisa appreciated that his manner might not mean chuckling politely at her chatter, but he had some gentlemanly impulses.

"Did you come for an apology?" Brisa touched her lips to draw his attention there and moved on to the next play in her playbook for the adorable apology. "I'm sorry. If you were here long enough, you know that everything I told you about Reyna was true. She is impressive. I didn't know she and Sean were falling for each other. I ended things as soon as I did."

It was the truth. The truth was always her final gambit.

"I came to meet her face-to-face, introduce myself. I don't quit as easily as you expected, and from everything I observed and our short conversation, your sister is exactly the kind of woman I'd hope to meet," Wade said. "You told the truth about her. I cannot fault you for that."

"I only forgot the minor detail of whether she was actually single." Brisa rolled her eyes and ignored the twist in her stomach at hearing another man, someone who wasn't her father, say her older sister was perfect. Reyna was great, but she wasn't perfect. She'd be the first person to tell him that, too.

If her sister found out that Brisa had tried this, that mildly disappointed frown that Reyna had worn for months after she'd come home would return, along with the expectation that Brisa would flake out on them in this new arrangement for Concord Court.

"I was still curious whether Reyna wanted a guy like me." Wade shook his head. "Or a date at all."

"I have excellent taste, Wade. The two of you would have been great together." Brisa frowned. She wanted to offer him something better than words, but what? "Can I apologize again? It was the old me. I can't make these mistakes anymore."

"The old you? From a week or two ago?" Wade tipped his head to the side as he considered that, and Brisa had to smile. He did have a sense of humor somewhere.

If he'd accept her apology, this mess could be untangled before Reyna or her father ever learned of it. Brisa would never do this again. No one would be the wiser.

Then the realization turned into a hard knot in her stomach.

"You didn't mention any of this to my father, did you?" Brisa asked, dread intensifying the fatigue until she sagged against the wall for support.

Wade frowned. "Of course not." His lips tightened. "You're exhausted." He ran a hand through his hair. It was longer than in any of the pictures he'd put on his profile, another reason she'd had trouble recognizing him. It suited him. His military cut had given him a hard, determined presence. Tonight, he was still determined, but he was also a hot laid-back guy in a suit.

"I am. I also understand that having good intentions doesn't change anything." Brisa shook her head. "Someday I'll learn that lesson and then watch out, world. I'll be unstoppable." She tried an honest grin. Men appreciated a woman who acknowledged her flaws, didn't they?

"I accept your apology," Wade said.

Relieved, Brisa relaxed. A gentleman. She wasn't going to have to plot and plan and recover from this mess.

"But forgiving isn't the same as forgetting." Wade bent to pick up her strappy sandals and gripped them in one hand before opening the door. "Let's go have a seat inside the bar. You'll be more comfortable there. We still have some things to discuss."

Brisa met his stare. He wasn't going to let her off the hook with only a heartfelt apology. Also, he had her favorite shoes.

She could listen. She owed him that much. She'd sit, have a drink, offer whatever help she could and gather enough energy to make it through the lobby and into a cab that would take her home. Alone.

When his hand settled in the small of her back, infusing her with a touch of his strength and a restless energy, Brisa fought off a shiver. On paper, Wade had been perfect for Reyna. In person, he was so much more.

CHAPTER TWO

WADE WAVED THE lovely Brisa Montero
ahead of him into the small, cool, dark bar
that took up the rooftop of the Miami Sandpiper Hotel. He quickly evaluated what he
hoped to accomplish by extending their
conversation. He'd had a plan. Introduce
himself directly to Reyna Montero and
make sure that Brisa Montero did nothing
to derail his courtship. Wade didn't want
to let Reyna slip through his fingers and
delay his goal. After a lifetime of wanting a
loving, stable family home, he wasn't about
to put it off any longer.

The brief taste he'd had was too sweet to
allow unnecessary distractions.

But then he'd seen Reyna Montero light
up in the embrace of another man and knew
getting the girl was no longer an option.

And getting even was a long shot.

Now all he knew for sure was that he

needed a new plan and Brisa Montero owed him. Maybe she could help him out.

As he watched Brisa tip her head up and shoulders back, he caught the scent of lemons or citrus. That surprised him. Something light and fresh, instead of what he'd expected—seductive, heavy and expensive. Based on the sparkle of pink dress, the impossible heels he was now carrying in one hand and the way her dark hair was elaborately twisted in a way intended to suggest messy and casual, he'd made a judgment early that evening that he knew her, understood who she was. Wealthy. Selfish. Careless, even.

That carelessness fit his original impression, too. After he'd read her confession about setting up a dating profile on her sister's behalf and texting him, all without her sister's knowledge, he'd been hostile and pretty angry. Wade had never met Brisa, but he'd decided immediately to correct that when Luis Montero had introduced himself and launched into a glowing description of his daughter Reyna.

Reyna was an unusual name, leading him right to her catfishing sister.

The opportunity to demand an explanation had been denied by unanswered texts. An opportunity to extract an apology could not be missed, then, even if it required a suit and mingling. He hated mingling.

But he'd listened to Brisa Montero's speech, tracked her as she'd worked the crowd smoothly and watched her stand up to Luis Montero, a man who inspired respect due to not just his monetary contributions to various causes, but his ability to bring others with him, to get things done.

Brisa was careless, but she was also tough.

He should have expected a curveball.

The fact that she'd corresponded with him on behalf of her sister put her in a category all her own.

Brisa might be the younger daughter, the most beautiful woman he'd seen in person in a long time and capable of reckless decisions like trying to find a match for her sister without permission, but she was smart. She'd been right about her sister being exactly his type. He'd watched Brisa move through the crowd and hold her own with her father's guests. He realized then that

she'd also charmed him right out of anger
and into…something else. She slumped in
her chair as soon as they found an empty
table.

"Mojito," Brisa said quickly as the waitress hovered. Her choice suggested the
drink was a need, not a want. For a split
second, as she'd been climbing down from
the stage, he'd seen stress on her face.

That had been before she looked his way
and when he'd decided to confront her. The
fact that she'd frowned as if she couldn't
place him had been a shot to his ego. Her
attempt to brush him off had solidified his
decision to demand a better explanation.

Her fatigue was already turning his determination to seek her into massive guilt
on his part. Her apology was all he could
reasonably expect, but Wade had never appreciated having his plans derailed. Even at
fourteen, when he'd entered his last foster
mom's house, he'd been certain he knew
how to make life work out correctly. Keep
his head down at home. Avoid all trouble,
so he could stay in the same school for the
whole year. Graduate high school, join the
Navy, build a career, be the best at that

career and have a family so he was never alone again. His failed marriage was the only flaw so far.

He was determined to succeed at each of those goals. All he needed now was the final piece of the puzzle.

The waitress pointed to him, a warm smile on her face.

"Ginger ale." Wade nodded firmly when both women paused and studied him as if they needed to confirm they'd understood what he'd said. He was comfortable with the reaction at this point. Two years of sobriety under his belt made it easier.

Brisa fussed with the tablecloth as the waitress walked away. "I've said I was sorry and I meant it. What else do we have to talk about? It's been a long week and I'm sure a handsome guy like you has lots of opportunities to meet nice women on that app."

Handsome. His immediate confidence boost was silly.

Wade stretched back in the tall club chair that he hated. Did these chairs ever fit anyone? He could sit, brace his feet on the floor and still couldn't rest against the back of the chair. What a terrible design. Brisa was perched gracefully. Of course, she was.

This place suited her. It was posh, overly expensive. He surveyed the tables along the fringes of the small dim room. Glass walls meant the city was the backdrop and at this time of night, the lights sparkled against darkness. Jazz played but not loud enough to intrude on conversation; the volume was meant to cover secrets being exchanged with the help of good liquor. This club was about atmosphere and romance.

It was not conducive to raking someone over the coals for lying.

Especially not Brisa. She flashed the megawatt smile to the waitress who returned with their drinks and handed her money, which included a generous tip, he noticed.

He'd certainly planned to be the one paying. Wade wanted control of this conversation.

Interesting. He'd misjudged her again.

"How is your ginger ale?" Brisa asked as she held her mojito to her lips. He couldn't read her face well, but he picked up a definite note of amusement in her tone.

Did she understand all the calculations happening in his brain?

He hadn't tasted it yet, so he sipped. "It's sweet. It's how I like it. Ginger ale-ish." It was. He'd grown accustomed to the drink, after trying and discarding several other nonalcoholic bar choices. "When you're sober and determined to stay that way, you learn to enjoy it."

"Oh," Brisa said. That was a common reaction, too. Before he could reassure her that he wouldn't relapse from absorbing any alcohol in the bar's air, she slipped out of her chair. "Let's find another place to talk, then. This isn't working anyway. I need to see your face."

She immediately swept through the cluster of small tables, drink in hand.

Wade grinned. This had been more of the attitude he'd expected. She would call the tune and men in her wake would dance. Still, it was a pleasure to follow behind, watching as she padded barefoot without a single hesitation across the hardwood floor to the hidden hallway that led to the elevator and the rest of the floor.

When Wade caught up to Brisa, she was pressed against a glass door.

"Perfect," Brisa said and she pushed open the door to step out under the overhang of a second, deserted bar. The pool glowed turquoise, and lights spaced around the edge of the rooftop illuminated several seating areas. During the day, the place would serve food and drinks to the hotel guests, likely families, enjoying the expansive pool. Tonight, the whole area was vacated.

Wade followed Brisa as she approached the edge of the pool. From there, he could see through the clear water to the bottom that sloped down gradually to a glass side and bottom that hung out over the Miami streets.

Glass. The bottom of the pool was glass. Nothing as reasonable or strong as good, old-fashioned cement. Glass.

His daughter was obsessed with having a pool.

He was glad he wasn't staying at this hotel and would do his best to make sure his daughter never visited. The argument they would have before she did a cannonball into the shallow end would give him an ulcer.

"How strong is glass?" Brisa muttered, shaking her head. "How is that a good idea?"

Hearing her assessment would have made Wade chuckle if they'd been about to discuss anything other than the matchmaking mess. He was gratified that she agreed with him.

Brisa moved to the wide shallow steps of the pool. There, the water covered her feet but nothing else. Her sigh confirmed his suspicions. The shoes were murder. Cold water was a relief.

Arguing with an exhausted woman with sore feet would make him a monster. Seeing her relax there on the side of the pool reminded him he was here to demand… something. The goal was fuzzy in his brain. Now that he was convinced Reyna was no longer a possibility, he needed a Plan B.

"Tell me how you decided I was the right man for your sister," Wade said. He couldn't forget what was meant to be happening between them, no matter how beautifully distracting Brisa Montero was.

"Okay." She nodded and took a long draw from the mojito. Her satisfied sigh was cute. That was dangerous. "I put the profile up on Military Match because my sister was returning here to Miami." She kicked at the water and did not meet his eyes. Was she concocting a defense or testing the water to see if that was enough to get her off the hook?

"What I want to know is why me. I already know what you did." Wade sipped his own drink. There was no justification for pretending to be someone else online. None.

"Our father…" She paused. "We have spent our lives fighting against his ideas for us. Fighting like running away from home to join the Air Force or marrying the high school boy who promised he'd never tell me no, and other small things like those. Recently, he'd convinced Reyna to come home to run Concord Court, but that wasn't her dream." Brisa rolled her eyes. "Even with our careers settled, he would have kept trying to match us to men who could further his dynasty. She needed a guy my father would never object to. Out of all the options, you were clearly the best. She would accept you."

The best. How? Wade considered that as he slipped off his shoes and socks and rolled up his pants.

"What are you doing?" Brisa asked.

"Testing the water myself. If the glass bottom falls out, the water may still sweep us out of the pool to our deaths, but I'm ready to gamble. Whoever chose an outdoor rooftop in the middle of August for a party must be cold-blooded." Wade slipped off his jacket and squatted to sit by the edge of the pool. He rolled his sleeves up and sighed when his feet hit the water.

"It's about appearance, not comfort," she muttered, and he had the suspicion she had chosen the location. "My sister solves problems. That's who she is. Her own, my mistakes, our father's cluelessness…" Brisa made a chopping motion. "She cuts right through to the heart of the matter and she fixes things." She took another sip of her mojito. "Reyna's been gone for so long that

I'd forgotten how that went. She wasn't even focused on the part of the equation I was working on, just went and fell for the guy I would have said was all wrong for her."

Wade twisted his glass as he considered that. Perhaps Reyna wasn't as far out of reach as he'd imagined, watching her lead away the guy, a happy smile flashing over her shoulder. "Wrong how?"

Brisa stirred the water with her foot. "Too charming. Too easygoing. He'd rather tease than argue and he picks up everyone around him. Props them up. Makes them stronger than they were alone. Sean's the kind of guy I'd want for me, not Reyna."

From that, Wade had to conclude that he was not charming, easygoing or the kind of guy Brisa liked. How did that feel? Not great.

He wasn't sure why there was a pinch in his chest near his heart. It wasn't that what she said was wrong. He wasn't those things. In Brisa's description of her sister, he'd found Reyna to be driven, ambitious and committed. Down-to-earth. That was how he saw himself.

Brisa valued charm in a partner for herself, but not her sister. Reggie Beaumont, the pro football star who'd hugged Brisa close before he left her all alone to deal with cleaning up, lived the life she expected. For sure Reggie had the money to move in the Montero crowd. Wade was a star in his own universe, but it didn't match Reggie Beaumont's.

"Dating wasn't on Reyna's to-do list. I'm not sure it ever has been, but I know what qualities she values. Duty. Intelligence. Leadership. A guy with accomplishments to match hers. I was right, too, because Sean has those things. I just…" She shrugged. "They've worked together for months. I've been right there with them and I didn't see anything that I would call romance. No extravagant dates. No flowers. No kissy flirting. How could I know this was happening?" Brisa asked.

Wade exhaled slowly. The woman he'd placed in the "Dating/Marriage" slot of his plan was otherwise engaged.

Brisa asked, "You didn't tell the whole truth, either, did you?"

Wade frowned. *What did that mean?*

"Because I wasn't living in Miami at the time?" That was the only thing he could think of. He hadn't mentioned his daughter, but Brisa didn't know anything about Thea. Not yet. His relationship with his daughter was growing. Talking about it too soon had seemed bad luck.

"Right," she drawled.

"It was a month. I expected us to correspond longer than three weeks. What's the hurry?" Wade asked. He'd been surprised when Brisa as Reyna had asked him when they could meet for coffee.

"Gramps, this is not the 1800s, no one has time for correspondence. No one wants to be texting back and forth for months. That delay? Boom. Sean makes his move," Brisa muttered.

"Well, I live in Miami now. I'll have a permanent address this week, as soon as you hand me the keys." Wade wanted to observe her reaction. He'd made a snap decision. He couldn't remember the last time he'd done so.

"At Concord Court?" Brisa asked, a small breathless squeak on the end. "Oh." Her brow furrowed deeper. "That's…" Her voice trailed off. She didn't know the word to put in there. He didn't, either.

Wade had a plan for Miami. When his newly married ex had moved here with his daughter, it had been a challenge, but he lined up a job at the hospital after his Navy retirement. He and Vanessa had worked out a shared custody plan, and after years of too short, too infrequent visits while he was stationed overseas, he could see his daughter every day. No more time zone challenges or unreliable technology or the weird space between them that grew over time and distance. He would build a home for his daughter. With his daughter. Concord Court would be the place to start.

"Your father made a big sales pitch on the place. I told him no." He had, at first, but he was reevaluating his answer. "I have a job, so there's no need for me to take up a slot someone else could use, but he insisted on me coming to the party tonight to see what Concord Court offered."

"And what do you think?" Brisa asked. Wade felt the twitch of his lips. She was concerned about his reaction to her project. That was dedication.

"I'm impressed." He was. How could he not be? "It's a good support for so many men and women. There's a whole community of people who need time to get their feet under them when they're first resuming civilian life."

She relaxed a bit. "Good. That's good. You know things are delicate right now, with my father and Reyna and what will happen. If you were to tell either one of them about our introduction, I'm afraid it might…" She bit her lip, an expression so powerful Wade had a hunch she'd used it often enough to know its effect.

"I'm clear on your problem and everything I can do to make it worse," Wade drawled. "What you don't understand is that I have my own problem. It would be smart to ask me how you might help if you'd like my support."

Brisa blinked as if she'd never expected that.

"A date? I could find you a date?" she said slowly. "I mean, that's your problem, right?"

Boiled down to the simplest terms, it

was. Was he about to expand on his plan, to complete her understanding?

She touched his hand. "Please let me help you. I am an excellent matchmaker."

He almost laughed. There was no way either one of them actually believed that.

He studied her face, waiting for her to admit the truth.

Her sigh brushed across his cheek, sweet and minty from her drink. "Except for you and Reyna, I have a good record." The shift of her eyes to the left suggested she was lying.

"You've matched how many happy couples?" Wade asked. The more they talked, the easier she was to read.

She sniffed and waved her hand. "Oh, I don't keep a running list." Because there weren't any of those couples. That was Wade's guess. "I have friends, pretty friends who would be happy to go on a blind date with a doctor, are you kidding me?" She tapped a deep rose-colored fingernail against her chin. "Narrowing down who to ask will be the problem."

Wade watched her think. "I know! She's perfect. I mean, you don't have a problem spending December in Aspen, do you? That's kind of a cute quirk, demanding snow for Christmas." Brisa held out her phone and then started scrolling through photos. "Let me do a better job of selling Jill."

Wade stared up at the dark sky as he pondered her words. The whole month of December in Aspen or a cute trip for a ski holiday? Weren't the holidays better at home anyway? That's what he'd always pictured, being able to hang stockings in the same place and putting the tree next to the window every year.

He wasn't sure, but he'd told himself those roots made everything better. This move to Miami was his shot at proving it.

Wade reached into his pocket and pulled out his own phone as Brisa held hers up with a flourish. "Tell me you don't want to buy this beauty dinner. I'll make reservations. I know a place that's booked for months, and the owner owes me a favor."

Wade paused his search through his own phone to study the photo Brisa had found. Jill was stunning, of course.

"Is that a real person?" he asked. She

was wearing a fur vest, fuzzy boots, and all of it was white. He wasn't sure if the background was Aspen, but there were horses and snowdrifts.

"Yes, she's a model. A successful one." Brisa winced. "Or she was the last time we crossed paths. Was it Paris or New York?"

"So, you're close, then," Wade said dryly as he held up his own phone. "I want to be matched with someone like her." He tapped the screen and she spotted Reyna's picture. "Not a model. A real person who has a serious job and reasonable expectations of travel plans."

"Models are real." Her lips thinned. "I have modeled, thank you very much. I am real, Wade." Then she sat back. "But I get what you mean. A woman with purpose, one with an important job, who pays her own bills and not by posing. Got it."

He should argue. He wanted to. Why did preferring that type of woman make him a jerk in this instance? Brisa's shoulders had slumped as if he'd hurt her, the most beautiful woman he'd ever met, and he honestly couldn't figure out why.

"Dating apps are a nightmare. If you can

find me a match using old-fashioned compatibility, we're even. That website? It's awful. So many options to choose from, and all terrible. No one talks. The pictures are fake or filtered. Down-to-earth. Easy to talk to. That's what I want. I won't mention the ad or the communication through Military Match to Reyna or your father." He wouldn't have anyway. What would have been the point? But Brisa had been afraid he would do that, so he wanted to reassure her.

Brisa relaxed again. On the surface, his ask was simple. Perhaps he should give her all the facts.

"I have a daughter. Your father wants me to be the example at Concord Court of vets who have families." Until tonight, Wade had no intention of being anyone's spokesperson, but the promise of making one element of his move to Miami simple was suddenly extremely appealing. Reyna was spoken for, reopening the frustrating search for a solid relationship prospect. If Concord Court met the basics and wasn't solidly depressing as military housing could be, it would cross one thing off his list, leaving more time for his daughter and his job. "Anything Concord Court can do to make the transition back to full-time family life would be helpful. I'll bring Thea with me for a tour of the facilities. If she approves, Concord Court will be my home for a while."

"We do have a list of requirements, a vetting process, you know?" Brisa tipped her chin up. "We tell you when you can move in."

He met the requirements. A job or enrollment in school. The end. Her father had been proud about how easy they made it to get support. "Right. I should talk to Luis, make sure I understood everything he expected."

Her eyes narrowed. Calling on her father was a mistake if he wanted Brisa Montero to like him.

Did he want her to like him? She'd lied to him and wanted him to keep her secret for no other reason than to be a nice guy.

None of that mattered. He did. He was. He wanted her to like him. That was something he'd need to watch.

"My daughter's opinion matters to me.

Veterans themselves aren't the only ones adjusting to a new life in these cases. You must know that. Concord Court could help with expanding services to support families with children and I'm all for that." She loved the place. His final point would seal the deal.

Brisa didn't argue. "Monday afternoon. We'll show you around. Not a word to Reyna about any of the rest of this." She held her hand out to shake.

Her hand was warm but delicate in his as he agreed. "Good."

"Do you have any other deal breakers? I mean, with respect to finding you the perfect match," Brisa asked as she stood. Careful flicks of her feet sent drops of water splashing in the pool. Watching her attractive legs as she moved was dangerous. Wade shook his head to rattle his brain back into thinking rationally.

"Really? None?" Brisa frowned as if she didn't believe him. "Another Reyna. You want someone with military background, obviously. Why sign up for Military Match otherwise?"

Because he'd been searching for the

woman who wanted him, one who was prepared to deal with his former and current
life. That was the most important piece.
Could he explain that to Brisa?

"A woman who has served will understand the challenges of making this relationship work. This second marriage needs
to last, and I want someone who's prepared
to go the distance." There. That made sense
without being sad. Wade stood and tried
to repeat Brisa's beautiful move to shake
water off her foot, but had to settle for two
quick kicks. She picked up her sandals.

"Military service preferable but not required, then." Brisa frowned. "You're so
sure you're complicated, only another veteran can understand? We've all got issues,
Wade."

Her easy dismissal was irritating. His
experience wasn't the same as other men
and women who'd served. No two were
alike, but they all shared experiences, some
very bad. Whether they were deployed into
war zones or provided support to those who
were, the demands took a toll. Those demands had broken his marriage and he'd
fallen right into a bottle. Brisa wouldn't

speak so carelessly if she'd known anything other than the charmed life as the daughter of a wealthy man.

But she'd braced one hand on his shoulder to slip on a sandal.

Citrus teased his senses while her warm weight shifted against him. When both shoes were on, she straightened her shoulders. "Fine, but I don't know enough retired female veterans. I'll need your Military Match log-in. We'll have to at least evaluate your options there. I'll screen the possibilities for you."

"But you won't be corresponding on my behalf." Wade picked up his jacket. "That's where this whole mess started."

Brisa grumbled, "No. Not for you. I wouldn't know how." Then she turned on a heel and headed for the door.

Wade waited for her to hesitate there. She didn't. She knew he'd follow her.

He caught up to her at the elevator.

"You know I'll never be able to find someone like Reyna, right?" Brisa asked softly as they stepped into the modern glass elevator. The Sandpiper knew its strengths.

Nothing impeded the view of the city or the ocean. "She's one of a kind."

Wade watched the floor numbers as they descended to the lobby. "I haven't met a woman yet who wasn't one of a kind. Help me track down *the* one for me."

He watched her eyes widen. "I'll do my best." The elevator had stopped.

Wade nodded and followed her through the lobby. It took longer than he expected because staff stopped her to ask about the service provided and the success of the party, and to give her reports on special accommodations she'd requested on behalf of some of her father's guests. Through it all, Brisa was patient. Sweetly appreciative. She remembered employees' names and what they'd done to help and mentioned that to the hotel manager who waited with her for a cab to pick her up.

Wade watched it all. He opened the door to the cab for Brisa to slide in.

Citrus was on the air as she said, "I'll see you at Concord Court."

He nodded and closed the door. The last image he had of her before the cab pulled away was the look of exhaustion he'd spotted on the roof for a split second. Being Brisa Montero was harder than it appeared, he admitted, but she was determined to do the best she could.

And so was he.

CHAPTER THREE

On Monday Brisa shifted behind the desk at Concord Court and tried to pretend she was completely comfortable in the hot seat. This was going to be her job, her place, her career. Eventually. All she had to do was convince one more person she could handle it. Her father was doing that thing where he studied her so closely that she felt like bacteria under a microscope and not the good kind that might lead to a scientific breakthrough.

Her sister was busy with the power of her own stare, poised on the edge of her seat. Brisa could tell she was ready to leap in front of whatever their father tossed in Brisa's direction.

"Postpone the small business lab. This is not the right time, even though I can't argue that announcing it at the party with my biggest clients was the perfect hammer to use against me," her father said, an annoyed frown on his forehead. "When I have more time, we'll come back to this. All of us. Your concept has value, Brisa, no one can argue that."

Hearing her father give her credit for something valuable slowed Brisa's response. Her father wasn't saying she, Brisa, couldn't handle it. He was asking to be included.

Wasn't he?

His approval, even if it was cautious, was too sweet to speed through. His advice was almost identical to her sister's. Reyna evaluated; Brisa went through life with her foot on the gas. It was frustrating to wait on what she knew was right.

Reyna patted their father's shoulder. "If I had to guess, your daughter is already halfway down the road to her first goal." When their father turned to his oldest daughter, Reyna surprised her by saying, "She reminds me of you that way. You listen, you decide, and you don't waver or look back."

Brisa cleared her throat and brushed down the khaki skirt she'd paired with the Concord Court polo. Wearing the official

Luis Montero–approved uniform had been an easy olive branch to get them off on the right foot.

But there he was, with his arched eyebrow.

"I have done preliminary work. Marcus Bryant was a huge resource in that area. He's a veteran here. Recently, he's been pursuing going into the design and landscape business with a friend. Understanding his challenges was one place to start building this program to support other vets who'd like to start a business on their own."

"One vet. That's your work on this?" Her father shrugged. "Good. Put it on hold, then."

"Show him the binder," Reyna snapped.

"How do you know I have a binder?" Brisa muttered as she reached down to pull it out of the tote bag she'd started carrying her first week at Concord Court.

Brisa slid the binder across the spotless desk. Reyna and her father leaned forward to flip it open.

"Phase one milestones," Reyna read out loud and pointed to the heading in case her father had missed it.

Brisa watched them scan the bullet points she'd written down. When the pain in her fingers caught her attention, she realized she'd tangled them too tightly together. Who did she think she was fooling with this binder anyway? She had no training, had never taken any business courses and had never graduated college. Starting a half dozen different businesses with no money and no goals in mind hadn't prepared her for something the size of Concord Court or the magnitude of launching a lab to support veterans opening small businesses.

"Funding sources," Reyna read and tapped the page after their father had turned to a new one. "She understands that you start with the money, Dad. Isn't that Montero philosophy?"

That had been the downfall of every plan Brisa had launched on her own. She'd expected her father to support her with his money. She'd finally learned that wasn't the answer.

"Licensing, city, state and federal guidelines and resources," Reyna read out loud and then scooted back in her seat.

"It's blank," her father drawled, as if he'd expected to run into this.

"I'm not moving forward without the resources in place," Brisa said, wanting to reassure him that her priorities were the right ones.

"Who are these resources?" her father asked and stretched back in his chair. Smugly satisfied. That's what she called this position. He expected her to fail his test.

"A lawyer. An accountant. Contacts at all the government levels." Brisa had known this question was coming. She'd tried to answer it while dozing last night, mainly because it distracted her from the embarrassment and unease at having Wade McNally show up out of the blue as he had.

Brisa pulled her hands apart and flexed her fingers slowly to return blood flow, while her father deliberated on what they'd said, his eyes locked on the binder.

Eventually, he made his decision. "I want a written report on Friday afternoon, close of business. In it, you and Wakefield will summarize the week's progress on the current ongoing projects and programs here at

Concord Court. We will meet on Monday morning to make a list of priorities. There will be no more secret projects. At the end of that period, we will launch this together." Then he motioned with his left hand. The "take it or leave it." Brisa had decided on that name for it the day she'd told her father she'd married her high school boyfriend at the courthouse. His offer? Annul and pretend it never happened or leave his house and bankroll for good. Take it or leave it. Agreeing to her father's offer never stood a chance against a cute boy who promised to always say yes.

Leaving home at eighteen had been harder than she'd expected.

Keeping a marriage alive to a boy who said yes to her, to his coworker at the bank, to their next-door neighbor and the bartender of his favorite hangout had been worse.

Returning and asking for her father's help at twenty-three had been even harder.

Offering his help with only a few good strings attached was progress.

"Dad." Reyna's tone had softened. "This is unfair. You never asked this of me. Please reconsider. BB and I can do this without you."

The jut of her father's chin was familiar, too. He was digging in instead of changing his mind. He would never change, so it was time to show her father she had.

Brisa took back the binder. "Fine. We'll call this a probationary period and it will last no longer than three months." Then she waited. This move had worked before with her other biggest, most-loved critic, her sister.

Her father's frown deepened. "Six months."

Brisa shook her head slowly. "No. You should be able to judge the value of my work in three."

The expression on his face altered a bit. She didn't have a name for this one. Had she ever seen this touch of curiosity? Or was it confusion?

"All right, but I want to be involved in the business lab. My expertise will be required," he muttered.

When his hand wrapped around hers, Brisa bit back a celebratory exclamation. Her sister's small grin and the hidden thumbs-up she flashed convinced Brisa she'd actually won. Again.

"What's on your agenda for the day?" he asked as he crossed one leg over the other.

As if he could hang out there with them forever. The satisfaction in his eyes was easy to read. Whatever his end goal, her father was pleased with their agreement.

This was unexpected. Hadn't he said he was too busy for more projects?

The flash of sun over the window's reflection on the long wall of the lobby caught her attention. "First, we'll help whoever this is coming into the office." She smiled broadly at her father. "Business as usual, Daddy. We love having you here, but we've got this."

He stood slowly, reluctantly, and nodded. "Let's get together for brunch on Sunday. All of us. Marisol misses you when we skip it." He'd stepped back from the desk when the door to the office opened.

When Wade McNally paused in the doorway to let his eyes adjust to the darker lobby interior, Brisa's skin tingled. It had been so embarrassing to have him ambush her at the Sandpiper, but she was going to have to cope since she'd be running into him now and then. That is, if he stayed.

WADE ENJOYED THE flash of cool air until he realized there was a group staring at him in the entryway. His daughter placed small hands on either hip and gave him a not-so-gentle shove inside.

"Hot out here, Wade," she stated matter-of-factly as she guided him all the way inside.

He must look like a statue on wheels given how she'd maneuvered him invisibly. He glanced over his shoulder. "You can stop pushing now."

The huff of air that exploded from her should have come from a bull ready for its matador, not a skinny nine-year-old girl wearing shortalls, a T-shirt and a NASA hat. "Okay, okay." Then she crossed her arms over her chest and channeled his ex-wife with a precision that had shocked him the first few times he'd seen it.

She'd been waiting on the steps when he'd stopped in front of Vanessa's house. Same stance. He'd been ten minutes late to pick her up for this trip. Thea was adorable, but she had high standards.

"Dr. Wade McNally, newest trauma surgeon in Miami, what a pleasure to see you today." Luis Montero swept across the cool lobby like a grand maître d' determined to do his best. "Did you have a chance to meet my daughters at our party?"

Wade avoided Brisa's gaze. "You made sure to tell me all about Reyna's accomplishments."

Reyna rolled her eyes behind her father's back. Wade clamped down on the smile, but it annoyed him all over again that this was a woman he seemed to connect with.

That convinced him to meet Brisa's stare. "Brisa and I had a short conversation about the amenities here at Concord Court. I wanted to get my daughter's opinion on the place. The new school year's starting soon, but she's got time today to check the place out." He braced his hand on his daughter's back and urged her to step out from behind him. "This is Thea. She's nine going on ninety."

"He tells that joke every time he introduces me," Thea grumbled. "Thank you for laughing."

Luis Montero frowned down at Thea as if he shared Wade's confusion about what might come out of Thea's mouth next, but then focused on Wade. "I'm so glad you're giving us a chance."

"Having your daughter here will be an excellent opportunity for us to explore programs that serve families," Reyna said. "That's something that I wanted to evaluate. All our current vets are single, no partners or kids here. We have the units, but it will take time, so if finding playmates for Thea is important…" Reyna trailed off. Brisa knew her sister didn't want to tell him that he'd have to think of somewhere else.

"I want a pool," Thea drawled. "You have a pool? We're set." She'd moved over to kneel down next to the dog sitting beside Reyna. "*Canis lupus familiaris*. Spotted coach dog." Thea and dog communicated wordlessly for a second. "And she's deaf. Interesting. I've never met a dog like this."

Wade hoped everyone in the room understood her puzzled tone was a compliment. Thea studied the world. When she met some new place or piece of flora or fauna, she was intrigued. Memorizing genus and species had been a hobby of hers since she'd learned to read. Eventually, she'd come to know more Latin than he did.

"Dottie's my dog. She works at a fire station. And you're right. She can't hear you. Sometimes she reads lips, though, and she never misses out on a treat." Reyna bent down to offer something for Thea to give to the dog.

He glanced at Brisa who was watching everyone quietly. Did she not like kids? She hadn't greeted Thea yet. Too bad.

"Is this cheddar?" Thea sniffed the morsel. "Cheddar cheese. Your dog treat is cheese." She held out her hand to the dog, who carefully took the food from her palm.

"It is. She likes a lot of different foods, though. What kind of treat would you choose?" Reyna asked as she ran a hand down Dottie's back.

"Cheese is acceptable. I'm a vegetarian. Lacto-ovo vegetarian. I like cheese." Thea repeated Reyna's brush down Dottie's back. "She likes that, too."

His little scientist.

"So happy you approve, young lady," Luis Montero said loudly and chuckled. "Thea speaks her mind."

Wade couldn't decide whether Luis believed that was good or bad.

Thea sniffed. "Thea does her research. If you'd like to live longer, I'll be happy to tell you how."

Wade froze as he evaluated his options. Telling Thea to be quiet was at the top of the list, but he was amazed at Luis Montero's mouth dropping open.

He must have been amazed, as well. Eventually, Luis said, "I should be going, let you get your tour started. I hope you'll choose Concord Court."

Luis Montero held up a hand in a general wavelike motion. "Report by Friday, Brisa." And then he'd swept out of the lobby.

No hugs. No future plans. No bragging on his other daughter, the one who sagged as if she was a puppet whose strings had been cut. Not every family was open with affection. He'd been through enough homes growing up to understand that, but he'd always wanted a hugging family. Right now, he and Thea hugged, but sometimes the distance between them kept him up at night.

Wade watched Brisa and Reyna share a look, their lips twitching.

"Should I handle the tour, BB?" Reyna asked softly as she stood in front of the desk. "I have plenty of time. I would like to encourage Thea to share any vegetarian tips she has with our father because watching his face scramble that way was amazing." Reyna held out her hand to Thea, who slapped it in a low five. "I like your style, Thea. Let's be friends."

Thea ducked her head and returned to conversing wordlessly with Dottie. The only time Thea lost words was when an attack of shyness hit. They didn't happen often around adults.

"No, I want to do this tour." Brisa met Wade's stare over the desk. Was she worried he'd spill the beans about her matchmaking scheme if she left him alone with Reyna? He wouldn't, but he could understand how she might be unsure of that. She didn't know him beyond a few pictures, his profile and their exchanged texts.

The memory of Brisa's dark eyes lit by the bar's candlelight and the conversation they'd shared while perched on the side of a glass-bottomed pool with a view of Miami's skyline floated through his mind.

Maybe she knew him better than he thought.

And she was going to help him with his plan. He'd get a place with a room for Thea. Together they'd start building their own traditions and make his place a home.

Having a good excuse to spend more time with Brisa improved his mood, Wade noticed. He might need to figure out why. Later.

Today he was going to be grateful for every minute.

CHAPTER FOUR

BRISA WASN'T READY to face off against Wade alone. The relief of escaping her first meeting in her new role as manager of Concord Court made it easier to pretend everything was good as she led Wade and his daughter through the pool area on the way to the unit she had in mind. The water shimmered in the faint breeze that stirred the tropical landscaping surrounding the pool, which made up the center of the complex. Miami's August heat fell back a fraction here.

She had helped design every inch of Concord Court. There was no reason to feel so out of place. That was a sign she'd had a hard discussion with her father.

"Thea, it's nice to meet you. I'm Brisa. Thank you for coming today." Brisa said to Wade's daughter as she double-checked the application Wade had quickly scrawled while they'd been in the office lobby. Reyna had hovered nearby, afraid to leave in case she was needed.

For an application and a tour.

Irritation had bubbled up, but Brisa understood that was always her sister's MO. To look after everything and everyone, including Brisa.

Wade's daughter shoved her hands in her pockets as she frowned down at the pool. "Why isn't anyone swimming?"

Brisa turned to Wade, the first time she'd gambled on making direct eye contact since they'd left the tension of the lobby behind. Why did it seem dangerous to meet his stare when they were together like this? He'd given his word not to expose their secret, and she had no doubt he'd keep it.

The danger might stem from the number of times his face had popped into her mind since she'd left him on the sidewalk in South Beach. As a face on a computer screen, he'd been forgettable. Nice enough, but not "forget why you opened your desk drawer" distracting.

Sitting across from him in the intimate

shadows of the cocktail bar and the memory of the way he'd watched her…

Like he saw her.

Not the face she showed the crowd, but her.

That had been hard to forget.

"Well, Thea, no one is in the pool right now…" Brisa clamped her phone in her other hand "…because the complex hasn't hit half its capacity yet and…" She had no idea how to answer that. Should they do something to increase pool usage?

"Grown-ups waste the best opportunities." Wade's daughter had her hands on her hips again. "A whole pool available for laps or practicing synchronized choreography or aqua therapy." Then she opened the gate and stepped into the shade. "Bougainvillea. My mom loves this stuff."

Brisa watched Wade's daughter rock back on her heels as she surveyed the rest of the landscaping. When she gave a satisfied nod, Brisa raised her eyebrows at Wade. Was she a proud grandpa in a preteen's body?

And what did she mean by "synchronized choreography"?

"Best I can guess is you're being evaluated on a pass-fail system." His lips curled. "You're doing fine so far," he whispered.

Brisa cleared her throat. "If you'll follow me this way. I want to show you the unit I think will be best for you, Dr. McNally. If it doesn't suit you, I brought another set of keys so we can keep the tour going. In this unit, your neighbors will be Reyna and Sean. These are the two-bedroom units on this side. You'll have one bedroom on the ground floor and one on the second floor, along with a second, large bathroom." Brisa fit the key into the lock and turned it. "I've got a pamphlet you can take with you, in case you need a reminder of the layout after you go."

Brisa pushed the door open and flipped the switch nearest the door. Overhead lights lit up the open-plan living room and kitchen combination. "Would you like a tour of the different features or would you prefer to explore on your own?"

When she turned back to get their answer, she realized Thea had already disappeared.

"She has zero interest in kitchens," Wade said as he stepped up next to her at the island that marked off the kitchen. "As long as it's meat-free, she's content." He studied the appliances—all stainless steel—and the cabinets—all oak with copper handles. "The finishes are higher-end than I expected."

Since she'd picked every detail, Brisa chose to take that as a compliment. "Concord Court isn't old base housing or a government-funded facility. This is a home. My father wanted classic but nice, something that demonstrated true quality. It's the least that veterans deserve." Brisa wrinkled her nose. "When you know how to get a deal here or there on granite, tile and flooring, it all works out."

"The designer did a great job," Wade murmured as he ran a hand across the smooth stone countertops. "Cooking here will be nice."

Brisa nodded, the thrill of his compliments, even though he didn't know he was giving them to her, shooting through her. There was something else, too. His hand on the stone made it easy to imagine him settled in, cooking a dinner. He would be good, never flashy, but solid, dependable.

Might wear a cute apron now and then and would always wash dishes as he went. Every meal could mean conversation and watching him work there.

And it was suddenly warm. Was she day-dreaming about a man in the kitchen? That was new.

"We should find out what Thea thinks of the ground-floor bedroom," Brisa suggested.

They found the girl spread out like a starfish on the beige carpet, staring up at the ceiling. "I'm thinking dark blue paint and some of those stick-on stars that glow in the dark." Thea raised and bent one knee, and crossed the other leg over it, gangly legs twitching as she envisioned her new room. "Yeah. Blue. I mean, purple could work or even black, but blue seems... acceptable, not too wild."

Brisa raised her eyebrows as she turned to Wade. He was slowly shaking his head as if he couldn't believe it, either.

"Not here, Thea." He cleared his throat. "Let's talk to your mom about doing that at her place. I'll buy you new furniture for there, too. You and I will do all the work while she and Steve are in Japan."

Thea's face had been lively before, full of curiosity and interest, but that changed in a heartbeat. "Right. Nothing fun like that here." She sat up slowly, resigned. "Never mind."

"It's just that…" Wade moved over to squat next to his daughter. Getting down on her level put their faces so close that it was impossible not to spot the resemblance. Father and daughter both had determined chins. "I don't own this place. When I buy a house and we move there, we'll discuss funky paint for your room then. Here, it needs to be temporary. Easy to take down when we go. Photos of Mars. Maps of the solar system. K-pop boy band posters." The last part of his speech was strained, but Brisa could tell he was doing his dad best.

She tried to remember her father ever bending down to their level when she and Reyna were girls to explain anything, and couldn't.

But today, her father had tried to explain his position. That had made conversation possible. Their father had listened. A succinct "no" had never gone well for the Monteros, either generation, but he kept trying it.

Thea nodded. "Mom said the same thing. They're renting the house. They'd need permission. Steve didn't want to talk to their mean landlady to get it."

Brisa had been enjoying the conversation until Thea's stare landed on her.

Like a challenge.

Was she the mean landlady in this scenario?

"You could give us permission, couldn't you?" Thea asked her.

This girl was completely innocent. Pure sweetness.

And the smartest one in the room.

"Brisa doesn't run this place by herself. I'm sure there are policies and she'd have to go talk to someone about making an exception." Wade sighed and stood, his knees popping loudly at the effort.

Brisa wanted to object. Was he trying to make her into the bad guy in all of this?

Even worse than the story's villain, he'd made her into the *weak* villain, the one who had to get permission. The fact that she'd almost agreed with him, initially…

Policy versus her father's special guest invitation.

A new twist on the "rock and the hard place" scenario.

Only one decision would make the little girl slowly blinking up at her happy.

Since Brisa could easily remember the time that she and Reyna had tried to re-decorate her room with some stars of her own, pink paint instead of blue, and had lost television privileges and their father's warm regards for an entire summer… Well, what else could she say?

"As long as you take the stars down from the ceiling and give the room a fresh, neu-tral coat of paint before you go, I'm going to give permission. No mean landlady here," Brisa said brightly. "I like an origi-nal design outlook. Maybe I'll drop by and be inspired."

Thea's fist pump in the air was cute. She might be a poor winner, but in this case, it was easy to enjoy.

"Pace off some measurements, Thea." Wade took out his phone and handed it to

Thea. "Make notes in my phone on the items we need, so we get the shopping done quickly. Count your steps from wall to wall. Corners to the windows and doors."

Brisa frowned. She was a little girl. Would she understand...

Thea immediately skipped to the corner and started counting steps, carefully placing one foot right in front of the other. "I'll do it twice to make sure I don't make any mistakes, Daddy."

"Very scientific," Wade announced and gestured at the door. Brisa stepped outside the bedroom to go collapse against the kitchen island. Her eyes met his and she had to clamp her hand over her mouth to still the giggles that bubbled there. He was a man who understood the depth of trouble he was in with a precocious daughter like his and it was adorable.

He put one hand on her shoulder to urge her farther away from the bedroom. "Do you see? I need another adult around here to help me ASAP." Wade covered his face with his hands. "Even two adults might not be enough to corral this child. This could be the origin story for some criminal mastermind, all because I couldn't outthink her fast enough. I tell her no and she outmaneuvers me. I'll be toast by the end of the week." She noticed his lips were twitching, and he had to cover his mouth with his hand, too. They stared helplessly at each other and laughed hysterically but quietly.

Finally, he slowed and said, "I like 'Daddy' so much better than 'Wade,' though."

When Brisa was sure she could breathe, she pressed her hand to the center of his back and rubbed a circle there. Until she realized what she was doing. His back. It was nice. Brisa cleared her throat. "You're doing fine."

"It's okay, you know. If you need to tell us no on the decorating, I get it, and she will, too." He held his hands up, palms out. "But it would be nice to have the cool bedroom, the one her mother wouldn't give her." Then he squeezed his eyes shut. "Petty. I'm not doing that."

Brisa straightened up. "Yeah. Don't fall into petty."

Wade sighed. "It's so hard. To have been the one who made do with phone calls and brief visits while her mother got to be in her life… I have to make up a lot of ground in a short period of time, and I'll do everything I can to make that happen, even paint and stick on stars." He shrugged. "Do you have any idea what it feels like to know that you don't quite measure up against someone else in the eyes of somebody you love more than life itself?"

The emotional punch out of nowhere caught Brisa off guard. Her knees shook before she managed a deep breath. Did she understand? She'd lived that for a lifetime. An entire lifetime.

But there was no way she could talk about that with him now.

Brisa cleared her throat and held out the key. "Welcome to Concord Court. We're going to do everything we can to help you and Thea feel at home here, Dr. McNally, uh, Wade."

His hand was warm as she pressed the key in his hand.

Whatever else she might have said in that moment evaporated as Thea jumped into the kitchen. One minute they were alone;

the next, Thea had landed in a crouch with a proud grin.

Kids were all over the place, weren't they?

"I'm ready to shop!" Thea said loudly, some of the maturity rolling away in sparkling eyes and wild bounce, as if the excitement was too much for her body to contain.

Wade raised an eyebrow at Brisa.

"Thea, you don't have a budget. Before we go anywhere, we're going to review your list of necessary items against how much we can spend," Wade said as he held out his hand for his phone. "Let me review your list."

"Five thousand should cover it, no problem," Thea said.

Brisa all but choked on the laugh she sputtered at his double take. "Five thousand dollars?" Wade exclaimed.

Thea pointed. "The place is empty right now, Wade. We need furniture."

His befuddled expression as he ran a hand through his hair was honestly adorable.

"Two hundred, not including furniture," Wade said. "Take three things off this list now. A fish tank is a want, not a need, Thea. I'm walking Brisa out."

His daughter's groan was loud, but she didn't argue.

Brisa walked ahead of him to the door. "Does every shopping trip always require a preset budget? This might be something I need to take into consideration when I'm setting you up." It was cute, but dating anyone who required that much organizing before doing the simplest things could be…a lot.

"I've missed out on so much time. I need to teach her about money," Wade said as he checked on Thea from over his shoulder. "No one ever taught me how to plan for expenses when I was a kid, so I made every mistake a person can make." She could tell that he'd worried about this and so many other things. "I want her to be smarter than I was. I want my daughter to have better choices."

His worry was sweet, but he was going to wear himself out. Parenting had to be a marathon, not a sprint. Wow. When she slipped and fell into sports analogies regarding a subject that she knew nothing about, it was time to go.

Brisa ran a hand down his arm. "For this week where you're moving in, you might throw caution to the wind. Have fun. Save teaching for another day." That would have thrilled her when she was a little girl.

Wade didn't answer.

"I'll leave you to it, then. Welcome to Concord Court, Thea," Brisa called out. "Wade." Shaking his hand seemed different somehow. They'd become more than business acquaintances, and his skin against hers was another connection.

It was definitely time to go. Wade McNally was handsome, smart and cared about his daughter.

Any intelligent woman would be interested in the former Navy man. Brisa would find him a great match in no time because the last thing she needed while her father was watching was a failed romance with one of the veterans she was supposed to be helping.

"I'll check on you both in a couple of days to see if there's anything you guys need." As Brisa left, she put on her brightest smile, ignored the urge to stay and closed the door behind her.

CHAPTER FIVE

ON THURSDAY EVENING, Wade answered the knock on his door with relief. He slumped dramatically against the door frame. "You're finally here." He waved a hand to invite his ex-wife and her husband in. "I was afraid she might do me in. We have argued over every single thing in the world that there is to argue about, and I keep losing."

Vanessa patted his shoulder while Steve offered his hand for a hearty shake. The chiropractor had the strongest grip Wade had ever encountered. Mustering enough strength to meet it took some effort. "We brought food." Steve twirled the pizza box.

"And a housewarming gift." Vanessa held out the plant she was carrying. "We already said our goodbyes to this pothos, so if you kill it before we meet again, it will know it was loved."

Wade accepted the plant. "Ha ha." He

moved to set it in a place of honor on the island. "Kill one beloved African violet with too much water, never hear the end of it." He opened the only cabinet that held anything and got his four plates, purchased on one of the countless shopping missions Thea had plotted. His budget idea? Smart but doomed.

"Mom, Steve, you made it!" Thea said as she bounced up and down. Her energy? Endless.

"Did you think we wouldn't?" Steve asked as he joined her in jumping up and down. They might as well have both been kids. Wade wondered if he should have some kind of routine with his daughter by now, one that expressed how happy they were to be together again. Steve and Vanessa had dated for almost a year before they'd gotten married, so it made sense he and Thea had worked out their relationship.

How long would it take before Wade and his daughter were as easy together?

Vanessa swooped in to save the pizza. "If you drop this…" The threat dangled in the air as she handed the box over to Wade. "Give us the tour, Thea."

After Wade set the pizza next to the plates, he followed them and managed to pick up the tail end of Thea's recitation. "...and the furniture will be delivered tomorrow, so by the time I come back, my room will be done." He watched her spin in a circle in the dark room while Vanessa stared around with less enthusiasm. The afternoon sunlight was waning, so Thea's room was shadowy.

"Isn't this kind of...depressing?" Vanessa asked. Wade was sure the question was aimed at him, but Thea answered. "No. Way! The stars are going to pop!"

Since he'd asked the same in a variety of ways and she'd said the same thing at regular intervals over the three days they'd been together, Wade added, "If Thea wants to make changes later, it's a coat of paint." That's what he'd been telling himself as he'd painted three coats to get the dark blue *dark*. Saying no would have been easier but watching his daughter light up with the new addition to her room was worth extra coats of paint in the long run. Their budgeting discussion hadn't made it far, but Thea had been his assistant for every project.

Hands-on DIY had to count somewhere for an important life skill.

"Let's get out of your dad's hair. He's exhausted." Vanessa ran her hand through Thea's messy hair. Wade had never passed his classes in braiding hair and Thea hadn't quite mastered the trick of getting a pony-tail to stay up. "He hasn't been in the Thea McNally training program for as long as I have. He needs to build up his strength."

Wade wanted to argue but she was right.

"Have some pizza before you go." Wade pointed over his shoulder. "We can sit in a circle on the living room floor and pretend we're camping." The suggestion had worked like a charm with Thea, but he'd been concentrating on the blessed day when his furniture would be delivered every time he'd had to climb back up off the floor.

"We've got another pizza in the car." Steve bent down to roll up the glittery sleeping bag shaped like a mermaid tail that had taken up the center of the bed-room along with a stack of plush cushions in the loudest colors the store had. Wade had planned to take his daughter home each night, so she'd have a bed to sleep in, while he'd crash on the couch. On their first night together, Thea had gone along with that until it was time to say good-night. Then, Thea had insisted on staying here. With him.

Finally, together, his daughter in his new home.

His home. Thea had two homes now.

Since that had made him feel at least ten feet tall and a puddle of goo at the same time, Wade had given in, and they'd made one more quick trip out and purchased tem-porary bedding. After that, his budget was officially history, not even a memory. His ability to say no had been vaporized, and Wade would remember the minute Thea had discovered the mermaid sleeping bag forever. There in the grim fluorescent light of the big-box store, her face had lit up with joy. Pink and purple and sequins had been more than she could have dreamed a sleeping bag would be. Making Thea happy was a high he'd be chasing for the rest of his life.

The moment had also been bittersweet because while he'd loved it so much, he hated the reminder that he'd missed so many others.

"Dad, don't forget. The bed goes over there by the window. I want to be able to stare out at night. You won't forget, will you?" Thea demanded. She bumped his side with her shoulder and wrapped her arm around his waist.

Caught off guard by how easily Thea hugged him, Wade hesitated but knelt and ignored the creak in his knee. He wanted to see his daughter's face. "I won't forget, but if I do, there's a drawing stuck to the refrigerator to remind me." Thea had taken planning seriously. Everything had been drawn to scale: the bed this many paces in a room this many paces wide. Her brain amazed him.

"Okay, the first thing we do when I get back is look at all my pictures of my vacation to Kennedy Space Center. Then we go swimming." Thea put her hand on his shoulder. "You should get some rest this weekend."

"Yes, ma'am." Wade nodded seriously before his smile bled through. Her tone had changed. In the beginning, she'd been unimpressed, remote, ready to go *home* home. It was sweet to know she was already making plans for coming back to this home.

It was easy to make his promise. Getting some rest was at the top of his list, as soon as his bed was delivered. Air mattresses might be better than hard floor but barely.

Thea squeezed him hard and then ran to jump on Steve's back, a move they'd perfected. Steve yelled, "Lift off!" before opening the door and running outside.

"Steve has missed his best friend this week," Vanessa said. "I've been forced to play horse every night Thea's been gone so he didn't wither away."

"I didn't know Thea liked basketball," Wade said and wondered how he'd ever learn all the bits and pieces of his daughter.

"I'm not sure she does, but Steve hopes to change her mind. Thea enjoys laughing at Steve, so he does whatever he can to entertain her." Her small smile was sweet, as if she found the duo exasperating but she loved them for it. "I hope she wasn't too…" His ex-wife shrugged.

It was nearly impossible to fill in the blank. He'd been lucky enough to spend long weekends here and there and at least one full week with Thea in the summers, but those days had been vacations, not everyday life. This week had felt similar but was so much more important. He wanted to make up for lost time, and so he and Thea had been running nonstop.

"I loved every minute of it. I've missed so much," Wade said as he rubbed the sore muscle in his arm. "But I am going to start taking vitamins. I should get the name of Steve's brand." Between the handshakes and the high energy, the guy was good for Thea and Vanessa, so Wade was going to do his best to appreciate that they all got along together.

"Can you handle two full weeks of dad duty? This honeymoon, the one we've delayed until now, is too important for you to fall apart on us. Toughen up." Vanessa bent down to stare up into his eyes. "Feeding the kid is the biggest hurdle right now. When school starts, things get interesting."

Wade saluted and watched her lips firm. She'd always hated when he treated her like a loudmouthed drill sergeant. "You'll be back in time. I'll pitch in any way I can. It was hard to do over the phone and with the time differences, but surely I can handle fifth grade reading and some math." Wade had no idea what their school routine was like, so all he could do was volunteer. He'd do anything to have more time with Thea.

"She's so smart, Wade," Vanessa said, beaming. "She doesn't need much help with things like that. Where I have to push is the social side, going outside the house, away from the computer, to meet kids. She's prematurely old for her age. If you have any ideas to help her make friends her own age as easily as she did the mailman, who has to be at least sixty and only happened to mention how much he enjoys hunting for shooting stars one time in passing and now hurries past our house in case Thea is waiting for him…" Vanessa sighed "…let me know."

"Of the two of us, I won't be the one to unlock that, V." Wade crossed his arms over his chest. This was another one of those arguments they'd had. She wanted a social life; he needed quiet. "I could check the library for a parenting book?" That was the best he had.

"There's a sleepover for the girls at

my neighbor Kathy's next week. She has a daughter going into the same grade as Thea." Vanessa shook her finger at Wade. "I convinced Thea to accept the invitation. I expect you to keep her from wiggling out of it. Can you do that, McNally?"

Wade saluted. "Sir, yes, sir. I will carry out your orders without fail. I will do my absolute best."

He hoped they were both clear that if Thea even hinted that she didn't want to go to this sleepover that Wade would buckle like bad roads in the heat.

Vanessa rolled her eyes. His best wasn't very good. "I liked the hug. I expected her to be calling me to come get her this week, but you ironed that out." She wrinkled her nose. "How bad are the fights?"

"Discussions, not fights. She does not like being told no," Wade explained.

His ex raised her eyebrows but didn't say anything. He could read between the lines. Vanessa knew exactly where Thea had gotten that from. He made plans. Those plans made sense. Arguing was a waste of time. He could definitely see the resemblance between himself and his daughter.

"As long as I agree to her ideas, no one shouts. I never imagined how much energy that takes, Vanessa. You've done a great job of raising our daughter without enough direct help from me." Wade wanted to say more, but as she had other times, his ex-wife waved off his thanks.

"You'll come with me to meet her teacher and her next visit to the pediatrician," Vanessa said. "She's going to be so much better off, now that we're all in the same city and we'll be staying in the same city. After the divorce, moving both of us home to Gainesville made perfect sense. My parents could help with Thea. Then I fell in love with another man determined to move me away from home. Steve promised no more moves. Miami is it. We're all putting down roots." She didn't demand any promises, just let him know what she expected.

"Definitely. I'll be here for whatever comes next." They both wanted what was best for Thea. Wade shrugged. "I mean, I'll be there unless the vitamins don't work. My stamina is not up to the demands yet of a nine-year-old."

They laughed and some of the worry lightened. Vanessa stopped with her hand on the doorknob. "Have you met your new neighbor who's moving in?" She waggled her eyebrows. "She's pretty." She drew the word out to emphasize *how* pretty.

"I have not. I saw the truck when we came in from the hardware store, but no one was outside." And it had been his third trip in three days. His daughter could take one thing and build like only one other person he'd ever known: his ex-wife. One idea led to another and all of them led to many home improvements. He now had a bathroom with a Milky Way shower curtain, although that had been a relatively easy battle to lose.

"Go introduce yourself. You can't expect every woman to chase you like I did," Vanessa joked. They'd met at a conference. Wade had been presenting; Vanessa was a surgical nurse and had been there for training. She'd approached him in the hotel bar with a terrible chemistry joke, demanded his number, and he'd made sure she had no trouble catching him.

Having that wife and the promise of kids

had been the next steps for him and her timing had been perfect.

Until he and Vanessa both learned that military life didn't work for her. Leaving her and his daughter behind while he was stationed elsewhere had nearly destroyed him, and divorce had given them new life as friends and family.

His next marriage would be completely different. It would be successful, for one thing. And for that to happen he was sure he needed someone who was or had been in the military, so they knew what he knew, firsthand. "I've never been good at meeting women." Wade gestured for her to step out on the small landing that led down to the sidewalk and the parking lot. "But advice to 'get out and try' from the woman who knows best what a bad bargain I am... Don't know what to think about that."

Vanessa slammed to a stop and turned to him with her eyebrows raised. "You? A bad bargain? No way. Life as a Navy wife? Dealing with your job and the hours and the calls? The loneliness and fear of you being taken from us? All the time away from your home? Watching alcohol take over… Okay, that was no walk in the park. But the things you faced, still face, and how you used to handle that…" She held up a hand. "All bad, but you deserve to find someone good. Someone who suits you more than me. We tried as hard as we could and didn't make it. I've seen how you're trying new choices. She's out there, Wade, and if she's as beautiful as the woman carrying boxes outside, you'd be twice a fool to miss out." Vanessa trotted back up the steps to hug him. "Don't be a fool, 'mkay?"

Before Wade could figure out how to answer any of the unexpected pep talk from his ex-wife, she'd made it to the car and slid in the passenger seat. All three of them waved as they backed out of the parking spot, and Thea turned around in the back seat to watch him until they left the complex.

Inhale slowly. Hold it. Exhale.

Wade closed his eyes and tried to regroup. Thea had taken over every minute, left him no time to worry about anything but the moment; here, from one second to the next, it was like his world dropped away. The empty present leaving too much bad history and fear that the future might hold failure.

He was alone again. After almost a lifetime of being alone, that should get easier.

The pain in his chest and the sting in his nose? Literal heartache.

Right now everything was scary and unknown and his ex-wife was encouraging him to ruin some other woman's life and his daughter was learning to love him and he had a big empty house to fill and a job to learn and no way to dull the sharp claws of fear except to make it through one minute and then the next.

Alcohol had been the pressure valve for his anxiety for a long time.

His plans were always about organizing, managing, controlling. Wade wanted control, but right now...

Learning to sit in that anxiety instead of immediately washing it away was a lesson he had to teach himself over and over. A good therapist had taught him the tools, but he still had to practice. At times like this, anxiety could drown him.

"Can anyone join in this meditation session or is it a private event?" Brisa asked softly.

Wade opened his eyes and found her standing on the sidewalk. While he was wearing a ripped T-shirt and paint-spotted shorts, Brisa was dressed in deep purple silk and linen and appeared as if she'd stepped out of a salon. Unlike their other meetings, he was at a distinct disadvantage here, but that didn't stop him from appreciating every inch of her style.

It was flawless.

"Sorry. You were standing there, so still, for so long, I was concerned." Brisa frowned. "That sounds like I thought you might need medical help." She cleared her throat. "What I meant is, everything okay? I'm guessing that was your ex-wife since she got in a car with your daughter and drove away? Hugging suggests things are good between you."

Wade considered that. He'd never reflected on how far he and Vanessa had come. Their divorce had been a relief, and he'd never blamed her for needing it.

"We're okay. She's a great mom." He smiled wryly. "Thinks I need to fall in love and soon. I didn't tell her that I'd had a plan for that, but someone derailed it."

Brisa nodded solemnly. It was impossible to maintain a grudge against the woman. But he still wasn't going to tell her Vanessa's suggestion. They were both quiet until he added, "It will take a minute to adjust since Thea left." He missed her. The faint ache he'd lived with since the divorce was stronger, more painful, and he hoped it was because he and Thea were closer now. Wade pointed at the truck. "Do I have a new neighbor?"

"Me. I'm moving in. Your least favorite person is now your neighbor." Brisa held her arms out. "My probationary period for Concord Court has changed. I need to be close to stay on top of all the day-to-day demands as manager, so I've decided to claim my spot here."

"Oh." Brisa was the "preeettyyy" new neighbor his ex had mentioned. Of course, she was.

"Yes, this is my sister's moving outfit." Reyna stepped up beside Brisa and brushed her hair out of her eyes. "You and I, we're dressed appropriately." She waved a hand to indicate their matching ragged outfits.

"Brisa is dressed like the queen is coming to dinner."

"Brisa is the queen," Wade said before he thought better of it. Brisa was so beautiful she didn't quite fit in the real world, she was more like a fairy-tale queen or princess.

"It's a tank and shorts," Brisa scoffed and pointed at her perfectly matched clothes. "Casual doesn't have to mean cotton."

"Whatever. I'm done for the day. I made your bed up so you can get some sleep when you're ready." Reyna mimed hugging her sister. "Don't want to spot the silk with my actual sweaty hands, BB. See you tomorrow." She nodded at Wade and walked down the sidewalk. In the next block of homes, Reyna's man from the cocktail party was sitting on the steps to another unit, Reyna's dog right next to him.

That must be Sean. Brisa had mentioned Reyna and him working together without any sign of romance. Wade watched the man stand to kiss Reyna slowly.

Apparently, romance had found them.

"Has better things to do than help me unpack, I see," Brisa muttered before turning back to him. "Joke's on her. I'm going to wait until she shows up tomorrow to do any more unpacking. I need food tonight."

"I have pizza but no furniture. I'm willing to share." Wade crossed his arms over his chest. This was a weird impulse. He wasn't sure where it came from except the prospect of returning to his now empty apartment alone. No furniture. No television. No Thea. Nothing to sway him from the worry that grew every day as his new job's start date drew closer.

That anxiety frustrated him. It was silly. September first would come, he'd report to the ER, and all of this worry would have been for nothing because he was good at his profession.

Telling himself that over and over was a weak solution. A distraction would help.

Brisa tilted her head to the side. "I would love to see the progress you've made with Thea's grand design." She took a step forward, but stopped. "If you're serious about sharing your pizza."

Wade turned and trotted up the steps to his door, a shot of energy kicking in. He was committed now. It was a slice of pizza. What could go wrong?

CHAPTER SIX

BRISA FOLLOWED HIM even as the Good Brisa in her head demanded an explanation of what she was doing. For days now, she'd been brushing away the thoughts that popped up occasionally about Wade and Thea. Why were they on her mind like this? Nothing good could come from getting more entangled in their lives.

She had too much riding on her success at leading Concord Court. Focusing on that was her priority. Wade's dating would be easy enough to resolve. She'd take care of that and leave Thea and Wade to their own devices. Distance was the correct answer.

But did she want to live in a world where turning down free pizza made sense?

"You weren't kidding about the furniture," Brisa said as she stepped inside. Almost everyone who moved in had bits and pieces, even if they didn't have a whole home's worth of furniture. Wade was starting from scratch.

"Delivery's tomorrow. I'll be up all night with the excitement, like a kid at Christmas. Thea has pillows, at least. We can borrow them for seats. I'm glad you're here. You might be able to help with something." Wade picked up two plates and the pizza. "Can you grab the drinks?" He motioned at the refrigerator with his head.

Brisa opened it and took out two bottles of water. The fridge was nearly empty. A carton of milk. Some juice. Not much to feed a growing kid or man. As she closed the door, a paper blew in the breeze. Since it was labeled clearly "Thea's Bedroom," it was easy to understand. Straight lines interrupted by gaps formed the outline of her room. "Bed" had been drawn in carefully near the window.

"If science and space fail her, Thea should study architecture or interior design, possibly both," Brisa said as she followed him.

Wade stopped in the middle of the dark room lit only by the twilight filtering through the blinds. "Computer, turn on the lights."

Warm light flooded the room.

"Whoa," Brisa said as Wade tossed her a big green pillow. She dropped it and took a seat. "That's new."

Wade grumbled, "The trouble with having a daughter who lives two decades in the future already is that her standards take real hard work to meet. Thea asked the guy at the home improvement store about 'easy-to-install smart systems' and this is what we ended up with. Lamps on smart timers controlled by the computer." He spread his arms out wide. "The future is here. Thea says that she needs to learn how to use voice commands because all space systems will be operated that way."

Brisa could read the pride on his face as he pointed out features of Thea's room. It was adorable. He'd worked hard.

"Now that I've figured out how to make this work, I have to consider Thea's promise that in ten years, every house on the planet will have its own brain." He raised his eyebrows as if he couldn't believe he was saying it, but it was hard to argue with progress. "Architecture, home design, space travel or designing RVs for weekend Mars camping, whichever direction Thea goes, she'll be prepared."

"I'll start saving my money for a Mars spa day," Brisa said. Then she added innocently, "Was the smart system included in the two-hundred-dollar budget?"

Wade scowled before he put two slices of pizza on the plates and handed her one. "I failed to teach her about budgeting. Over and over, in fact."

Failed to teach her. Did he think he only got one shot?

"Is that sausage I see?" Brisa asked. "What did the vegetarian say?"

Wade pointed at the pizza. "Gift from my ex-wife, I'm guessing. They had another pizza in the car. I bet it was Thea-approved."

"Sweet. Neither one of you would order her dinner and tell her to like it, whatever it was, would you?" Brisa said and took a bite. Now was not the time to remember how many times she'd choked down yogurt at breakfast because her father insisted it was the healthiest choice before school.

Anything with the consistency of cold mucus had better be super healthy.

She hadn't touched the stuff since she'd married Hartley Amis and moved into his off-campus apartment.

"No," Wade drawled. He frowned as if he was trying to figure out where the question had come from. "Why would anyone do that? Do people actually do that?"

"Force kids to eat things whether they want to or not? So many people, Wade." Brisa tried to imagine the battles over the Montero dining table if she'd demanded a special diet. It would have been intense. Her father against Reyna, while Brisa wished she'd never brought it up.

His confusion was sweet. Forcing his daughter to eat something she didn't like made zero sense to him. Naming the emotions hitting her from all directions would take a minute, so Brisa ate while she watched him chew.

"Thea is determined. For now, she's made a vegetarian choice and it isn't a whim. She will tell you all the advantages to herself, to me, to the planet. I don't know that anyone could talk her out of it."

Brisa remembered her father's face in the lobby. "If she persists in explaining how it leads to long life, Luis Montero will do his best to correct her."

Wade groaned. "I'd almost forgotten Thea's smart answer to Luis. I should work on manners, speaking with elders, too."

Brisa chuckled. "Oh, if you could somehow get Thea to call him an elder..." She held her side as she laughed at the image in her head. Eventually, she realized he was grinning at her but also watching her closely. "Manners are good. Knowing how to put someone who is being rude in their place, though? Priceless."

Wade didn't answer immediately. "Truth is, I'm almost certain I've created a monster. This room is her vision. The bathroom's got a solar system shower curtain." He sighed. "I've started calling this a suite and 'Thea's Galaxy' and I'm afraid she'll annex the living room next. My credit card statement will tell a sorry tale."

His dry delivery made it impossible not to giggle again.

"She's lucky. I love to see a man wrapped around his daughter's finger. Teaching her about money can wait. We all learn how to manage it sooner or later. You did. I did, sort of. Figuring out who she is has got to be way more important for both of you."

Brisa didn't meet his eyes. Concentrating on her pizza was easy. When she didn't look up, Wade cleared his throat.

"So, I mentioned my furniture delivery tomorrow, but I've been called in to the hospital for a mandatory orientation." He crossed his legs. "Any chance someone could let them in for me?"

Brisa took another bite as she nodded. "It's my day off. I can do that."

When he didn't answer, she glanced up from her pizza to see him frowning. "That easy? You just volunteer?"

She frowned to match his. "Sure. I can do it. It's simple enough. I've seen the important architectural drawings already. So…" She pointed in what she hoped was the general direction of Thea's drawing on the refrigerator. What was the big deal?

He nodded. "Okay. Thank you. That's nice of you on your day off. I hoped someone on the maintenance crew could help."

Brisa shook her head. "It's a small operation now, but that's kind of the goal I have for Concord Court. I want anyone who needs help to come to us. If we can provide the answer, we will."

Wade's frown faded, but she had the uncomfortable sensation that he was rethinking his opinion of her and she wasn't sure what that meant. It had to be an improvement, right?

Then he reminded her of the agreement between them.

"Any news on the date you're going to find me?" Wade asked as he stretched out and plopped the last bite of crust in his mouth. "My ex-wife may decide to hunt up her own candidate if I don't find someone soon."

Brisa picked off a piece of sausage and squeezed it between her finger and thumb. "Really?" Wade and Vanessa were close. Hartley wouldn't answer her phone calls the last time she'd tried to contact him, and when she'd run into him at brunch at her father's club, he'd stared right through her. He'd adjusted to life away from their parents' money better than she had, but he'd never gotten over the need to sleep with the prettiest female in the room. Every room.

If they'd had a baby together, would they have been friends? It was hard to imagine.

Wade picked another piece of pizza up. "I don't know if she'd set me up, but she wants me to get out and date. I'm glad Vanessa doesn't hate me. She has a right to."

The urge to blurt *Why would you say that?* was strong. Being curious about his past was another bad sign.

"Did she have someone in mind? A good possibility?" It would be nice if his ex could take care of Brisa's obligation and she could go hide behind the desk in the lobby until Wade McNally was safe and secure with some other nice, dependable, good-for-a-family woman.

"Well, the way she drew out the word *pretty*—" Wade copied her delivery "—when she mentioned the woman moving in next door made me think she was suggesting you."

Brisa blinked slowly as she tried to determine his reaction to that.

He was studying her face and giving nothing away.

Did the military train people to do that? Her sister could be unreadable at times, too.

Brisa whistled loudly and enjoyed the way he winced. No one ever imagined she could whistle like that. "Could turn into a mess, dating a neighbor like that, couldn't it? Besides, that woman? She's a mess. You want a hero. Good thing I'm your least favorite person in Miami."

There. Lighthearted. That was good. Nothing to indicate how something had shifted inside her at the suggestion of Wade focusing his attention on her.

When she managed to check on his reaction, he was staring up at the ceiling. He didn't face her when he asked, "Want to see the coolest part of the room?"

"Yeah," Brisa answered, relieved the subject had been dropped.

"Computer, nighttime setting," Wade said, his voice gruffer than she remembered.

The warm yellow light of the lamps blinked out and white twinkle lights lit up in swirls along the wall. The glow-in-the-dark stars stuck to the ceiling were faint, as if they were on the edge of the galaxy.

"Wow," Brisa whispered. Magic. Wade had created magic for his daughter with paint and lights and hard work.

"Pretty good, right? The girl is clever." The pride in his voice was clear.

Brisa realized she was having trouble breathing. The emotion in his tone. The gift of this room created by and for his daughter. What she would have given to have that kind of relationship with her father. The sweet surprise of finding a man who was implacable on the surface but goo on the inside for one little girl...

It was too much.

"I almost hate to go back to my boring, unmagical place," Brisa murmured as she forced herself to stand. "I may hire you and Thea to do some work there next."

"Give me five or six years to recover and I'll consider it," Wade said as he rolled up to stand next to her. "My knees will never be the same."

Brisa laughed softly because that was what fit in the space of their conversation.

Then she turned on her heel and scurried for the door.

And she would have made it except he said her name.

"Hey, Brisa, catfishing and dashing my hopes of the perfect Reyna aside, there's no way you're my least favorite person in Miami. I don't want you to leave here believing that." Wade shoved his hands in his pockets. At least he was as uncomfortable with the emotion as she was.

"Good. I'm glad. Come by the office on Monday, and I'll tell you about the date I set up."

His eyebrows shot up. "You set it up already? Without talking to me."

Of course, she hadn't, but by Monday, she would. She needed to get them both moving in different directions. She had Concord Court to run; gasping for air at the love for his daughter would change her focus. This was her last chance to show her father, to show her sister, she could do this.

No man could distract her.

"She's perfect. Wait and see." Brisa darted out the door before he could ask her any more questions.

Why had she lied about having this date planned?

Bad habits were hard to break.

She didn't want him to catch her in a lie again.

Finding him a date had to move to the top of her priority list for more than one reason.

CHAPTER SEVEN

ON FRIDAY AFTERNOON, Wade followed the HR liaison to his new office and tried to remember the woman's name. Something that started with a *K*? She was tall, blonde and fast. Working in medicine led to being quick on your feet. Apparently, HR was the same.

"Here we are," she said as she pushed open a door and turned on the lights. The flash across her name badge made it easier to read. Whitney. No *K* anywhere in her name. He had such a way with women.

Whitney stepped inside. "You're all set up. In your binder, you'll find some basics on navigating the hospital's computer system, but you'll get more information on that from IT. There's some general information, a map, hours of the cafeteria service, things you might occasionally need and all the forms you have to fill out. You can call if you have any questions, but please let us know your decision on which levels of vision and dental insurance you'd like as well as all the optional products like short-term disability by the end of the month. Anything I can answer for you now?"

Not now that he'd read her name tag. Whitney. Her name was Whitney. Everything she'd rattled off? He was going to need time to untangle. Wade shook his head.

Her smile was beautiful, open and friendly. "Take it all home. Read it over. Call me and we'll set up an hour to go over everything you're interested in and forget the rest. Okay?"

"I appreciate that. I'll probably need some advice." Wade returned her smile. Friendly. That was his goal.

She squeezed his arm. "Welcome to Miami. If you need suggestions on neighborhoods or restaurants, don't hesitate to pick up the phone. I'd love to be your guide." Her cell rang, so she pulled it out of her pocket before scowling at the display. "I have to take this. I mean it. Call me, Wade."

Then she was hurrying back down the hall.

Wade dropped the heavy binder on the bare desk in his new small office that was buried on a dead-end hallway and inhaled slowly.

Change had always been hard for him.

And this was going to be a big change.

Plus, he was almost sure that Whitney would like to go to dinner at one of the restaurants she could recommend if he worked up the nerve to ask her out. Why couldn't he breathe right? He pressed a hand to the heaviness in the center of his chest.

Years in the Navy had meant plenty of new places and faces, but the backbone of structure and command had been there to fall back on. Whether he'd been stationed in North America, Asia or Africa, naval command changed direction like a tanker at sea, slowly and only with lots of room to maneuver. Here, everything was bright and shiny and fast. So much was open to interpretation or special knowledge he wasn't sure he had.

"Surgery will be the same," he muttered to himself as he moved to sit behind the desk. Pulmonary failure, cardiac failure,

blunt trauma, internal hemorrhaging...
none of what came through the emergency
room doors was predictable, but he knew
the process of evaluating the options to
save a life. He trusted that knowledge.

Feeling so far out of his element was
sometimes a precursor to an anxiety attack. Having one in his new place of em-
ployment would never do. Sometimes he
could talk himself down. The sweat form-
ing at his temples was a sign meltdown was
imminent. "You know surgery. You're one
of the best in surgery. Years of experience.
Nothing changes that." He closed his eyes
and focused on his breathing pattern again.

Trauma surgery was stressful. Neither
his alcohol addiction sponsor nor his therapist had ever fully understood how anxiety
faded when he was faced with the problem
of how to treat a gunshot wound or someone hurt by explosion or fire.

He had to get out of his head when a life
was on the line.

Unknowns like hospital accounting,
billing procedures and navigating the em-
ployee benefit system threw him for a loop.
He hated unknowns. In surgery, he had a

wound. He had this many possible solutions. He understood them fully. He decided and moved to the next crisis.

Here, none of these decisions meant life or death. Every choice was fine, some better, some more expensive, which made comparing them difficult. Adding a pretty, interested woman out of the blue was one choice too many. He wasn't ready for this.

To slow his elevated heart rate and improve his shallow breathing, Wade stretched back in his chair, jerked at the loud crack and then settled again to study the ceiling tiles over his head. He had to count each exhale. As many times as it took.

When his heart rate finally slowed and he could no longer hear his pulse, Wade sat up. Fatigue swamped him. As soon as his muscles relaxed, the panic receding, exhaustion hit as if he'd been in battle. The back of the chair remained at an incline. One hard yank from him brought the chair back to its upright and locked position.

"Who do I call to fix that," he wondered as he flipped open the binder to find the computer log-on instructions. Wade rested his forehead on his hands as he scanned the table of contents.

Wade had a meeting next week with someone from the hospital's IT staff, but he wanted a look around. He'd only worry until everything was clear to him and this was something he could address. His nurse assistant would also be coming in. Wade had no idea how Antonio Vargas had been chosen or by whom, but his achievements were solid. That was one piece of the scary puzzle that fit.

Wade traced a hand down each step of the log-on as he worked and relaxed against his seat when the system responded perfectly. The loud crack warned him, so when he was facing the ceiling again, Wade shook his head.

The knock on his door distracted him from giving the seat back another hard yank.

Luis Montero stood in his doorway, a frown on his face. "Having trouble with your chair, Wade? That won't do."

Almost everyone Wade had been introduced to called him Dr. McNally. Luis

Montero assumed they were closer than that, apparently.

"Yes, I'll have to call…someone to get it fixed or replaced. It's not the first time I've inherited somebody's hand-me-downs. That's the way of the world. New guy misses out on the frenzy of trading up when someone leaves an office." Wade waved a hand toward the armchairs with ratty blue-gray upholstery. "Why don't you try one of those chairs? I can't guarantee they're safe, but we won't know until someone gives it a shot."

Luis paused with one hand on the chair. Then he raised an eyebrow and perched carefully.

When it held, Wade said, "Oh, good."

He'd meant it as a joke. It wasn't a great joke, but Luis's unreadable reaction suggested he didn't view placing his trust in an unreliable seat to be a humorous matter. Did Montero find anything funny? If Wade had been the guy to make snap judgments, he'd have guessed Luis Montero was the type of man to hire someone else to take the risk of a faulty chair first.

His daughters were very different from this Montero.

"Was there something I could help you with, Luis?" Wade asked, returning Montero's use of his first name with pleasure. If the older man wasn't going to stand on ceremony, Wade would follow his lead.

"Just dropped by to make sure everything is going well," Luis said as he pulled his phone out of his jacket pocket. Without pause, he scrolled through numbers, made his choice and put the phone up to his ear. He nodded at Wade while he waited for his call to be answered. "Trina, I need you to call Dr. Holt on his cell. Let him know that the office assigned to Wade McNally won't do. Then pick out a good desk and chair, nice ones, leather, expensive, and have them delivered next week to McNally's new office. Yes, use my personal accounts." Luis listened for a minute. "That's all for now." His smug grin as he dropped his phone back in his pocket was irritating.

"We'll get this sorted out next week, Wade. I'll get it taken care of. No need to worry about the chair or this small office." Luis stared at the room. "Trina will choose some artwork, too. Expensive but simple subjects. A bowl of fruit, perhaps. Maybe flowers." Then he waved his hands. "No need to thank me. We want you to be happy here. And as a board member of this hospital I have a special obligation to look after you. Now, is there anything I need to address at Concord Court? How is your daughter settling in?"

Mindful of the state of his chair, Wade braced his elbows on his desk. He'd spent a lot of time around military commanders, men and women secure in their spot at the top of the food chain. They ordered; they didn't ask. Luis Montero might not have any military service under his belt, but he'd mastered the attitude.

"Brisa has done a great job of making sure my move into Concord Court has been easy. Seamless, really. I wasn't expecting my orientation today, but I couldn't miss it. Brisa is meeting the guys delivering my furniture for me on her day off. Very hands-on. Helpful. I needed that today especially." What an understatement. If he'd been forced to reschedule and face an empty bedroom when he made it home after this day, he might not be able to breathe his way through a meltdown.

He owed Brisa Montero.

Wade wanted to make sure that Luis Montero knew that Brisa was good at her job. He recalled his annoyance at the memory of Brisa's muttered complaints about her father's lack of recognition for all she did…

"Good. Good. I'm relieved to hear you've been treated well." Luis frowned. "We're in the middle of a transition. I do hope you'll let me know if you run into any challenges while we come to new terms at Concord Court. I hadn't expected this when I raved over the level of excellent service we provide, but I will make sure it is maintained."

There was something off about the whole situation in Wade's judgment. He didn't know Reyna well, but Brisa had responded quickly, efficiently, every step of the way. What did her father fear would happen and why?

He remembered Brisa referring to herself as the messy one in the Montero family. Barring the catfishing incident, he hadn't seen any evidence of a mess. Wade realized it was a big exception, but he'd let it go. Grudges had never been his style. Growing up in foster care had taught him to process and get past whatever he was feeling as quickly as he could.

"Now that Brisa is my neighbor, it should be even easier to address any minor questions I have." Wade couldn't imagine what Luis expected might go wrong. The townhome complex was new, but running well thanks to Brisa.

"Your neighbor?" Luis straightened in his chair.

Did he not know his daughter had moved in?

"Yes, she moved in this week," Wade said.

Luis shook his head slightly. "I warned Reyna not to allow that. When Brisa changes her mind and leaps to the next wonderful opportunity she sees, getting her out will be a hassle and then we'll have to spend time, money and effort to prepare the unit for someone else to move in." He considered his phone again. Was he about to make another phone call? To Reyna, to fix the problem? Or to Trina, to hire an eviction crew? "I should have made this a condition of her probationary period."

Montero's world-weary air of a man who had been there and done that all too often grated on Wade's already frayed nerves. Wade hadn't spent more than four hours total in Brisa's company, but in that time, he'd observed her pride in Concord Court and the fine work she was doing there.

A good father should be supporting that, not loudly expecting her to fail.

As soon as the thought hit, Wade wondered when he'd determined what made a good father. He'd never had one. Up to this point, he hadn't been one, either.

But he knew he was right.

Wade started to ease back in his chair, remembered at the last minute that the seat was broken, and decided to stand instead. "I've been impressed with both of your daughters, Luis, but Brisa has done the most to make sure I have the support I need in this move. I don't have the history you do, obviously, but I will say, from where I stand, she deserves more credit."

He'd intended to be firm but nonconfrontational. The way Luis's lips firmed into a solid line suggested Wade had overstepped the mark.

Handling personalities like Luis Montero's took skill, no doubt.

The hospital wanted Wade, though. Luis wanted him at Concord Court. That gave Wade room to maneuver.

Luis stood and straightened his suit coat. "I am glad all is going well at Concord Court. Luckily, I do know both of my daughters. If one should falter," he said as he raised his eyebrow, leaving no doubt which daughter he meant, "the other will step up. And, of course, I am keeping a close eye on our new manager's standards." He winked and held out his hand. "As a father, you may one day understand that our children need our direction, no matter how old they are. Our duty to protect them never ends, Wade."

Wade stared at the hand for too long. Was he going to shake it?

At that moment, he could remember Brisa's face when she encouraged him to forget teaching to have some fun with his daughter. It was hard to imagine Luis Montero buying a mermaid sleeping bag.

Eventually, he accepted the handshake but tried to add some of his ex-wife's new husband's power to his grip. "I'm still figuring out how to be a *good* father. I haven't had a lot of time in Thea's life until now, but I hope I'll know when to protect her and when to step back and let Thea be Thea." He let go of Luis's hand, hoping he'd made his point.

"She already speaks her mind freely, doesn't she, Wade?" Luis smiled. "Young fathers. Get back to me when her dream has changed from vegetarianism and becoming an astronaut to flying jets in war zones or the fifth failed business, the second broken engagement to men who had once been important clients or after a disastrously silly marriage to a mere boy, and an investment of millions in a townhome complex that can change lives. You may understand then that only firm guidance can keep them safe."

Wade propped his hands on his hips as he considered that. Luis had a valid point. Wade didn't have much experience under his belt.

But Wade did have the fresh memory of

Thea's easy hug, and her boundless enthusiasm. He didn't want that to change.

"Well, you might be right, but I hope when she comes to me with excitement in her eyes about whatever it is, whether it's twinkle lights or pictures taken by the Mars rover, or this boy or that job or…whatever, I'm going to want it for her, too." Wade hesitated. "I never had a father to tell me yes or no, so I made my own decisions. Eventually, my daughter won't need me the way that she does now, if I do my job correctly. This is my only shot to convince her to come to me when she does make the wrong choice. I had no one, Luis. I don't want that for Thea."

That was the worry that kept him up at night. He never wanted his daughter to feel as alone in this world as he had. She could be smart and strong, but that wouldn't protect her from the fear that came with being on her own.

He hadn't been able to dig through all the lists of things he wanted to tell her, show her, give her to protect her until this moment, standing across from Luis Montero. The man was looking at him with a mixture of pity and anger and something else Wade couldn't name.

"No, you don't." Luis sighed. "I did have a father, one who took his job of teaching me to be a man seriously. He prepared me to come here and make something of myself. Cuba is so close, but my father couldn't come here to save me from my mistakes. His lessons were hard but here I am, a success beyond his dream for me. I have given my daughters everything I can. All I want to know is that they will be successful, safe, secure." He shook his head. "We are fathers. We teach our children. We protect them while we can. We worry when we cannot."

That honesty bled through Wade's irritation. Luis's words came from the heart.

Luis stepped toward the door. "I believe we have the next two weeks to get you all situated, is that correct?"

Wade wanted to argue, but he was so tired of shopping. He should insist on buying his own working desk chair and artwork.

Trina probably had great taste. She passed Montero muster.

"Yes, I'll start shifts at the hospital then." Wade rubbed his forehead. "I would appreciate your help, Luis. Setting up a whole new life has been overwhelming. I didn't think I needed Concord Court, but I have to admit having the decision on where to move and getting through all the steps required, so easily, has been a huge weight off my shoulders."

Luis met his stare. "I'm glad. I know Brisa will be, as well. Concord Court is important to us all because it is a way to give back to the men and women who have risked so much. If we can improve there, I hope you will help us do so." Then he left.

The footsteps faded and Wade plopped back down in his chair and carefully tipped back to stare at the ceiling. "I'm going to sleep for two days straight." He was tired.

But he'd accomplished a lot so far to re-establish a life for himself, and for Thea, even if the unknown was still looming.

He understood Luis Montero better now. He was a father who was confused by his daughters. In that way, he and Wade were alike. Luis was holding them close and tightly, exhausting himself in the process.

Wade wished that would work with Thea, but not even Luis Montero was successful with that technique.

And he'd learned more about Brisa. She saw the strings her father held tightly. Did she understand why they were there?

He liked them both a lot more.

The urge to step into the middle of Montero family drama was strange, he realized, but Wade knew he'd do it again for her.

CHAPTER EIGHT

ON FRIDAY NIGHT, Brisa had nearly hit her limit for time spent with her big sister. It had taken a lot, but being bossed by Reyna step-by-step over the course of an afternoon had accomplished setting up Brisa's place. However, having Reyna's help unpacking after the move across town had proved to be too much of a good thing. Brisa bit her tongue and tried to be grateful for the extra hands. Since the number of boxes remaining had dwindled to four, Reyna had to run out of steam soon.

"As soon as we finish the kitchen cabinets, we'll move on to hanging pictures," Reyna said as she dried the final plate, slid it into place and picked up Brisa's phone. "I'm going to text Sean to bring his tools. He should have locked up the office already. We've made so much progress since I got here."

Brisa pasted on a pleasant expression as she wiped her hands dry. Her manicure was shot. Avoiding dishpan hands had never been too big a challenge, thanks to dishwashers, restaurants and fast food, but Reyna had been determined every dish, pot and pan should be washed before it was put away.

A clean start, she'd called it.

And, since Reyna had the perfect plan for the most efficient layout of the kitchen, her sister had been the drier, not the washer, even though Reyna had never once sat still for a manicure in her life.

Brisa spread out the wet dish towel and concentrated on her sister's best points. That would be enough to swallow her complaints.

"We don't have to do it all in one day, Reyna. Instead of putting Sean to work, why don't we all go out somewhere? We could get some food, some drinks and relax. My treat, to express my appreciation. Everyone has worked a full week, you know." Brisa motioned at her outfit: jeans and a new T-shirt advertising Hometown Rescue. The animal shelter was their partner in the Shelter to Service dog training program Sean and others had started at Concord Court. "I'll even wear this out in public. You know you want to see that. You can take a picture to remember it always." Brisa reached up to smooth any loose strands of hair back up into the sleek high ponytail she'd chosen for that day.

Reyna's eyebrows shot up. "You? In a T-shirt? In public? And not at an event for the shelter?" She squeezed Brisa's shoulder. "Are you feeling okay?"

Brisa shrugged her hand off. "I'm tired. I know you're not, but come on, let's take a break." Even she could detect the beginnings of a whine in her voice, like the kid in the toy aisle who wants this one thing, just this one toy, she promises, and she'll be so good. Dinner. That's all it would take to sweeten her mood again.

Reyna nodded but she was frowning down at Brisa's phone. "Sean's on his way." She scrolled with one finger and in that second, Brisa remembered the notifications she'd been getting off and on, ever since she'd logged in to Military Match to search for a great date for Wade. A panicked grab for her phone was denied when her sister spun away. They'd played this game ever since they were kids.

Coming up with a reasonable explanation would be a good idea.

It was too bad absolutely nothing came to mind.

"A dating app is surprising. One filled with veterans instead of wealthy jet-setters is even more puzzling." Reyna stopped in the corner of the room and waved the phone. "But these are all women. Is there something you need to tell me, BB? It's fine if there is." Her sister crossed her arms over her chest and waited.

"I'm helping a friend out. He wants someone to take a shot at making a match for him, and I said I would." Brisa carefully schooled all the individual pieces of her face to reflect zero emotion. No lie could be detected that way. At the base, her answer was true. No one needed to know that she'd dug the hole for herself and was only attempting to climb out without getting in even deeper.

Her big sister had never been able to tell a lie. When Reyna tried, it immediately ate its way out from the inside. Brisa had never understood that. While *lying* lying was bad, white lies made the world a better place. White lies smoothed misunderstanding, soothed hurt feelings and basically made the wheels of society turn.

This lie? It was gray, but she was comfortable in the gray.

"Is it someone who lives here, BB?" Reyna asked. "Because I don't know that either one of us is qualified to add matchmaking to the selection of services Concord Court offers. Is that even an actual service that anyone provides?" She frowned. "This is weird. There's something you aren't telling me. What is it?"

Brisa marched across the room and yanked the phone away from her sister. "It's not that much weirder than a friend saying 'hey, if you know any single women, could you set me up?' in my opinion." She scrolled down, eliminated every single woman who'd responded by the number of filters and amount of skin showing in the photos.

Another Reyna. That was Brisa's goal for Wade.

Brisa also found a missed call from Reggie. She'd return it later.

Reyna pointed her finger at Brisa. When they were younger, that would have been enough to start a fight, but Brisa had grown past that. Pretty much. "You aren't telling me who it is. Why?" She stopped to study Brisa's face. "Sean, your good friend and someone I could see asking for your help, is out of the question because I will torture you both if he's searching for my replacement already. Peter Kim is dating someone new every week and doesn't need your help. Marcus..." She nodded. "Could be him. You guys are good friends, working on the new business lab together."

Immediately picturing Marcus's response if Reyna mentioned this search to him, Brisa shook her head. She needed his assistance too much to gamble on losing it for a weak alibi. "Not Marcus."

Reyna didn't answer. Eventually, she would land on the right guess. Her sister was too smart to fool for long. Distraction was Brisa's only hope to buy time.

"Food, Reyna. I need food." Brisa shoved

the phone in her pocket and turned up the whine. "I'm starving. Don't make me beg."

"Oh, the drama," Reyna muttered. Before her sister could follow with whatever firm, encouraging, "get yourself together, Brisa" speech that was building in her brain, the doorbell rang.

Brisa went to answer it, but Reyna held up a hand to stop her. "I've got it. Sit."

Thankful, Brisa slipped onto a kitchen stool. Sean entered, holding up a tool bag. "I'm prepared." He set it down and wrapped an arm around Reyna's shoulders to pull her into his side. "Are the Montero sisters fighting or did I miss the explosion? You've been together a long time with no chaperone."

"I had hoped Brisa was going to hit me with a revelation about her love life. Instead, I find out she's dabbling as a matchmaker." Reyna suddenly slipped out of Sean's hug. "Hey, as if we can't get along for a few hours without you to run interference."

Brisa had to laugh.

Sean's slow grin was sweet as he reached for Reyna again. Her hesitation was so brief that it didn't matter. Reyna melted back into his side and said, "You got here just in time. We were about to go there. I'm being bossy again and the whining has started."

"Of course, you are being bossy," Sean said and pressed his lips to Reyna's forehead. "That's why we love you. Sometimes we want to put you on a slow boat leaving the bay, but we always love you."

Brisa hoped she'd get used to seeing the two of them together like this. It was still so new, and while they were in the office, Reyna and Sean each had their roles and acted professionally. But after work, they were so cute it was hard to spend time with them while she was as single as single could be.

Except for Reggie.

She should definitely call him back when she had a minute.

Why did the prospect of calling a handsome, wealthy, nice guy weigh on her like a burden?

Would she ever find someone who matched her as perfectly as smart, easygoing Sean matched her smart, fierce sister?

"What if…" Sean held his hands out.

"Go with me for a second. What if I hang the television? Then I take you both out for seafood?" He pointed at the tools and the bracket for the television. "Everything I need is here and I don't have to listen to the two of you arguing over the placement of Brisa's photos of Brisa."

Brisa stood slowly. "They're pictures of famous landmarks, you twerp. Some people travel. Some people take photos of the places they visit. Some people even hang them up to remind them of good times they've had."

Sean pursed his lips. "Some people don't place themselves front and center while the Eiffel Tower is pushed to the side and cut off in every single pose, but okay."

"My sister is a model, Sean." Reyna propped her hands on her hips. Sean and Brisa both knew this was her fighting pose, a warning. "If those other people in the picture were as beautiful as she is, cameras would frame them the same way." Her sister was using her dangerous voice, the one she employed when someone was being mean to her little sister or when her little sister was maybe, possibly, being a bit over-the-top.

That was the reason Brisa needed her sister, bossy pants and all.

"I love your compromise, Sean," Brisa said as she wrapped her arms around her sister and squeezed her tight. "It's two against one. You lose."

Reyna rolled her eyes. "Fine. I'm hungry, too. Don't think I've forgotten the match-making mystery. Let me work on it and I'll find the answer to who your bachelor is. I'll finish the bathroom. You two get the television set up." Then she spun on her heel and disappeared.

"That's what we said," Sean muttered as he picked up his bag. "But you just have to get the last word in."

"I heard that," Reyna yelled from the bathroom.

Brisa and Sean exchanged a quick smile. "The TV goes here," Brisa said as she pointed at the longest wall. "I'll be able to watch it from the kitchen, too."

Sean nodded. "Good." And that was it. He didn't need any more guidance, and Brisa had no urge to supervise his work, so she reconsidered changing her clothes. She was under no obligation to wear this outfit out in public now.

She'd turned to judge her chances of slipping past the bathroom to get to the bedroom when someone knocked on the door.

Seeing her "boyfriend" Reggie on the steps was a surprise. "Hey! What are you doing here?"

"I called. When you didn't answer, I decided to make the trip over." He motioned carefully with his left shoulder and cut his eyes that direction before holding up an extravagant bouquet of flowers. "I had to see the new place."

Brisa stepped out to hug him for whatever photographers were nearby and then took his hand to pull him inside. "Come on in."

When the door was closed, Brisa took the flowers. "Where did you pick up paparazzi tonight?" Thanks to her sister, she knew exactly where her vases were in the kitchen. She sighed as she ran water into a vase and dropped Reggie's bouquet in, because no matter how often she complained about Reyna, Reyna was always proven correct. In this case: it pays to be organized. It was so annoying.

"Hey, Sean," Reggie said and then craned his neck toward the hallway, "and Reyna. Good to see you."

Sean nodded over his shoulder, his hands full of television, while Reyna darted out to hug Reggie and made kissy faces at Brisa before ducking back into the bathroom.

"They've been following me since I left the stadium. I had a meeting with management about my contract." Reggie surveyed the living room and kitchen. "I've almost got the terms I want, and every bit of good press reminds everyone how much I bring to the team. This is my last shot before I retire and I want it all, three more years to play and an agreement to add me to the coaching staff. I'm pushing for ten years in total. They want me, but that ten-year request has them hedging, so it's time to turn up the heat, add some public pressure from my fans. You up for a night out on South Beach? We could get dressed up." He motioned at her casual outfit. Reggie was already in a suit tailored perfectly for him. "You know the photographers are waiting to get a shot of you in a sexy dress. Cameras love me, so gossip sites love me, and the team loves any good publicity these days. Let's go dance some. It'll be fun."

Brisa hesitated. She could hear Reyna in the bathroom, and Sean fixing up the TV. Saying yes to Reggie had always been so easy. She loved dressing up and dancing. When Reggie was focused on her instead of making deals, he was a lot of fun. People stared and pointed. Drinks flowed. Everyone had a good time.

It was like being a celebrity without all the baggage.

But after a full day of unpacking and Reyna, and so much else, all she wanted was…not dressing up or dancing. In fact, the idea of putting on Brisa the Party Girl made her instantly fatigued. What she wanted was comfort food and to relax. Immediately.

While she framed her answer, she and Reggie ignored Sean's muttered curse as the cords on her television tangled as he was trying to mount it on the bracket.

"Can I get a rain check?" Brisa asked

as she tried to untangle Sean as best she could. "I'm a mess tonight."

Reggie tipped his head to the side, mild disappointment fluttering briefly across his face. "Sure. Those guys have a picture to work with. Should get you some exposure for your shelter, too." He motioned at the door. "Walk me out? I wanted to get your opinion on something. And this time, we could do a quick kiss for some insurance that we make the news."

Annoyed, because she was clearly busy, and now reconsidering the merits of a pretend boyfriend to annoy her father, Brisa dropped the cords. "I'll be right back," she whispered to Sean. "Do not drop my television." His grunt was the best answer she'd get, so she moved around him to open the door. Reggie wrapped his arm around her waist as they stepped outside. Brisa turned to make sure the T-shirt could be read plainly in any photo that was taken.

"Sorry I missed your call earlier," Brisa said as she leaned against him. From a distance, this could be a sweet embrace. "I'm glad negotiations are going well." Reggie was great. He had big dreams for the next phase of his career in Miami. She was happy to help in any small way.

He pressed his forehead to hers. "I'm worn-out with all the back-and-forth. I want it done so I can play ball, no worries." When he raised his head, he said, "Would you be okay with helping me accelerate this process?"

"Yes," Brisa said, "let's definitely plan a big night out. I'll find a fundraiser, we'll dress up, I'll drop hints around the room to every powerful person I know about how you and I both want to keep all your charisma and care for the community in Miami, which you do."

Reggie squeezed her closer. "Good, good, good. What would you think about doing all that with an engagement ring on? We could make a big splash now, then when the season starts, realize we make better friends or something, blah, blah, blah." He fluttered his lashes at her. "It's a winning plan."

The faces of her angry father and devastated stepmother flashed before Brisa's eyes. Another broken engagement would be proof to them that she was stuck in her old pattern. Brisa wanted to break free of that pattern.

"Let me think about it," Brisa said. She wanted to be loyal to her friends, but the hard knot in her stomach made it impossible to agree immediately. He had his eyes on his goal; she had to consider what this charade would do to her own.

He nodded and they did their quick kiss. It was pleasant. They'd gotten pretty good at pretending to be a couple.

"Call me when you want to go dance," Reggie said as he squeezed her hand. He trotted down the steps and had backed his sports car out of the parking spot and left Concord Court with three cars trailing behind before she realized she'd left Sean holding a large piece of electronic equipment.

Brisa turned to hurry inside, but heard Wade calling from his steps, "Hey, Brisa."

She peeked inside to see that Sean had put the television back down on the floor as he did something to the wall mount.

When she turned back, Wade was on the sidewalk in front of her. "I wanted to say thanks for meeting the furniture delivery guys. It was a long day at work and…" He tugged on the loose tie dangling around his neck. His clothes were as bedraggled as she felt. "It meant a lot to find that couch as soon as I opened the door." He pointed at the parking lot. "I should have come sooner, so you could introduce me to Reggie."

Understanding that he'd seen the kiss settled heavily in Brisa's mind, but she wasn't sure why it mattered. It had to be a good thing, another sign that they belonged with different people. A fake engagement would cement that division.

Why didn't having that obstacle between them make her feel better? She knew her relationship with Reggie was for show, but Wade didn't. His expression was friendly, but she could read the long day in the slump of his shoulders.

Since she understood well how hard it was to move into a new place, Brisa waved off his thanks. "I'm glad I could help." A hard thump reminded her that Sean was performing a delicate maneuver with her television all alone. She pointed over her shoulder. "Come inside?"

Wade followed her up the stairs.

In the living room, Brisa realized she was watching him closely. Too closely. Closely enough that she could see fatigue around his eyes, as if he hadn't been sleeping, and something else. Worry, maybe.

If she'd had to guess, she would have assumed someone like Wade McNally strode through life confident in every situation. Was she wrong?

"Sean, have you met Wade?" Brisa asked. "Sean works here at Concord Court, keeping the place up and running. He's also the creator of the rescue-therapy dog project here. Oh, and he's dating Reyna."

Sean held the TV awkwardly. "I would shake your hand, since Brisa chose this second to make introductions, but, uh…"

"Let me help." Wade shrugged out of his coat and moved over to where Sean was mounting the television. Neither one of them said a word, but the operation was seamless. Reyna joined them.

When the television was up, the remote control had been tested and all the connections to her collected electronics were set, Sean sighed with relief. "Nice to meet you, Wade. As I understand it, you've had an impressive career, and Miami is lucky to have gotten you. Luis expounded at great length on what your presence here could do for Concord Court." He held out his hand.

Wade shook it. "Luis Montero is either the world's greatest hype man or he needs more to concentrate on."

"Why not both," Reyna said cheerfully. "I'm happy to share the limelight." Then she patted Wade's shoulder. "A man who steps up to help, Brisa. Did you notice?"

At Wade's raised eyebrow, Brisa huffed out a sigh. "Reggie would have done the same thing if we'd asked. He needs a nudge, that's all." Always. Reggie also needed a nudge to drag his attention away from his phone and his deals and promoting his image.

Her sister's harrumph had to be ignored because she didn't want to get into a sister discussion with an audience, and she was so close to food.

"Oh, is Reggie the bachelor you're setting up?" Reyna asked as she clapped with excitement. "Because that is a fun game I want to play." Then she wrinkled her nose. "Not through Military Match, though."

"Military Match..." Wade repeated. With horror, Brisa watched her sister tilt her head and study Wade carefully. The slow smile that spread across Reyna's face was confirmation. Unless Brisa could find a convincing story, Reyna knew that Wade was the bachelor she was helping.

And if Brisa wasn't careful, Reyna would keep pulling at the string until she unraveled the whole story.

"We were about to head out, Wade." Brisa tried to make a clever, sneaky motion at the door that shouted, *Make a run for it and I'll distract her*, but it was a lot to ask a single head motion to convey.

"Have you eaten? Come with us. Sean introduced us to this hole-in-the-wall seafood place. They have cold beer and good shrimp." Reyna brushed her hand across Brisa's shoulders. "And Brisa will finally blend in for once."

Brisa's eyes met Wade's, but she wasn't sure what message she wanted to send.

If he said no, she stood a better chance of throwing her sister off the hunt with...

something. She'd figure out the rest of it on the drive.

But he was tired. Worried. And alone.

Why she wanted him to say yes should be examined. Later.

Wade held out both arms. "Am I overdressed?"

Sean nodded. "Yep, but if you don't mind being hit on by every barfly in the place, I wouldn't say it's a problem. Honestly, I should put on a tie and head down there myself."

Reyna narrowed her eyes. "Oh?"

"There it is. My favorite expression." Sean stepped up to her and kissed her lips. "Unforgettable."

They both laughed. Brisa and Wade rolled their eyes. Couples with inside jokes. What could be any grosser than that?

Reyna jingled her keys. "I can drive. Brisa is dying. She needs food." Her voice was a bratty imitation of Brisa's, and Brisa had a flash of all the times she'd been desperate to have her sister home. Why was that, again? It was hard to remember.

Wade bent to whisper in her ear, "When

they step outside, slam the door and lock it. We'll order a pizza for the two of us."

It was sexy and sweet, and the two of them sharing their own inside joke.

Brisa had to close her eyes and shake her head. The temptation was real.

"It's good food. Don't worry, we'll ditch them after." Then she reached for his hand and pulled him out the door.

CHAPTER NINE

WADE WASN'T SURE about Surf and Turf when Reyna parked in front of the place. A long weathered boardwalk leading up three flights of stairs to what appeared to be a mix of a biker bar and a deserted shanty. It sat out on a pier over marsh with hanging mangroves. The closest neighbors were expansive nursery farms and...nothing else. Streetlights didn't make it out that far, and it was hard to find where dark land met dark water.

Because it was *dark*.

The drive had reminded Wade of locations on TV shows where the bad guys lure cops in order to double-cross them and hide their bodies. The road was bare, making it so easy to imagine a collection of Florida's natural predators might be perched beyond the headlights.

There was no traffic ahead of them or behind them.

But the parking lot was full.

Surf and Turf was off the beaten path. It was almost off the map completely.

The fact that business was still booming suggested this was one of those places only locals knew.

And that the food was worth the adventure.

Wade was glad to have the escort. If he'd decided to make the drive himself, he would have turned around at the first creeped out shiver that went down his back. He still might. He could climb back into the car and wait for whatever fate befell the rest of the party. Staying up late to watch old news stories about the number of boa constrictors and pythons slithering around South Florida had been a bad idea. Yes, Thea would think it was cool when he told her about it. But finding one in the dark out here? Less cool.

"You still back there?" Sean called out over his shoulder as he and the others trotted up the flight of steps leading to the gray, weathered building with neon signs advertising cheap beer and good food. "Did a gator get you?"

Brisa glanced over her shoulder. "Ignore him. You're safe."

"Oh, good. No gators? I keep hearing plops that make me wonder," Wade muttered as he took the final step. He wasn't sure what noise gators made just before they had dinner, but the plops had sounded...large.

"No, there are definitely gators, but it's the snakes that creep me out." Brisa grimaced. "If you come during the daylight, you'll see them. They're well-fed so they don't present much of a problem."

Much of a problem. Wade froze as he evaluated that. It wasn't exactly reassuring.

Neither was the way Brisa's lips twitched. Was she joking...or not?

Sean pulled open the door and motioned a group of five women out. "Ladies, y'all have a nice evening."

Every one of them had spent time in the salon having her hair set and styled into fluffy curls that week, and their outfits fell into a pastel range of comfort wear.

Not bikers.

Not tourists.

Grandmothers in the mood for cheap beer and tasty fish tacos, apparently.

And not too scared of Florida's reptile population to chance dinner at Surf and Turf.

Wade had spent more time than he wanted to remember in bars all over the world. Some of the memories were hazy, thanks to too much whiskey, but the places were usually dark and loud. So was Surf and Turf, but it was also different.

The woman propped up against the podium straightened as soon as Sean stepped inside. She would have fit in most of the dive bars Wade had visited. She wore black head to toe, T-shirt, jeans, boots. Her salt-and-pepper hair was twisted into a severe knot that left impressive ears exposed, and the lines on her face had probably been made from smoking too much and staring into the sun.

But her welcoming grin was pure brilliance. "Sunshine, I ain't seen you in weeks now. Your grandmother been keeping you busy? What's Mimi got you doing?" She pressed a kiss to Sean's cheek, wiped the smudge of bright pink lipstick off his cheek and led them through the large crowded room cluttered with tables. When she made it to the back corner, she pointed. "Sit. I'll bring y'all your usual." Then she pinned Wade with a hard stare, and he realized he was holding her up.

The line of her eyebrows suggested slowing her down was a big mistake.

In a hurry, Wade slid into the booth next to Brisa and checked for a menu.

Until he noticed everyone was watching him.

"It's real simple, 401(k). Surf or turf. Them's the choices." The woman narrowed her eyes at him. "Don't give me no trouble with any special requests, you hear."

Reminded of the ominous plops that might or might not be alligators outside, Wade nodded. "Yes, ma'am. I'll have surf. Please." He tried a smile. "Thank you."

"And a beer." She nodded.

"Actually, Cookie, I've been telling him about the power of your sweet tea. That stuff would sweeten up any bad day. We'll both take a shot of sugar, please." Brisa grabbed his hand under the table.

Wade wanted to explain that it didn't bother him to have to explain to every person he met that he was sober. Had to be sober. It had become such a habit that he couldn't let it slow him down.

Her eagerness killed the response. Brisa was trying to help him. She'd cared enough to remember their first meeting and step in to smooth over any awkwardness.

Wade met her stare and then nodded. He hated sweet tea, but he'd drink it happily to see her face light up with pride and concern, all for him.

The woman swept the table with a careful gaze before shrugging. "Sweet tea? Fine by me, Cover Girl."

When Legs was out of earshot, Wade heaved a deep breath and reached down to roll up his sleeves. "Is it hot in here?" Nerves had turned up his temperature.

"Cookie has got a good bluff. Making men sweat is one of her favorite pastimes. You did fine," Reyna said. They all straightened as their waitress slid drinks into the center of the table and disappeared before anyone could acknowledge her.

"It gets easier when you're part of the

family, like Sunshine here." Brisa handed Wade a tea and nodded at Sean.

"What can I say? My grandmother brought me the first time. I never looked back." Sean sipped his beer. "That's Mimi. She makes friends wherever she goes…" Sean nodded.

"The food here is great, Wade. The nicknames…" Reyna wrinkled her nose.

"So, is Cookie her nickname…or her real name?" Wade asked.

"Nobody knows for sure." Sean gestured helplessly.

"Sean is Sunshine." Wade turned to Brisa. "And you're Cover Girl. I get that." She was the most beautiful woman he'd ever met. It made sense that her nickname would call that out.

He turned his icy cold glass in a circle. "401(k)?" He flipped his tie. "I guess the nickname could be worse, but I should have mentioned I'm a doctor, so she would have given me something like Scalpel or Bone Saw… You know, a surgeon's tool with an edge would have been cool."

When everyone laughed, Wade realized he hadn't heard Reyna's nickname.

He studied Brisa's sister across the table and tried to imagine the positions reversed, he and Reyna the couple while Sean and Brisa watched. The picture wouldn't form. Reyna and Sean had to be a couple, even the way they moved was in sync. Would he and Reyna have ever gotten along that well? Sean was funny, easygoing.

No one had ever described Wade as either. He pointed at Brisa's sister. "What does Cookie call you?"

Reyna wrinkled her nose. "Reyna."

Wade frowned and turned to Brisa. She would get his confusion and explain it.

"Honestly, Cookie calls her Reyna and puts some respect behind it." Brisa squeezed his hand. She hadn't let him go. Wade was happy with that. "You will learn that normal rules do not apply to Reyna Montero."

Thanks to their history, he and Brisa could have a private conversation in public. Her answer was light enough, but she was explaining something more than nicknames, too.

Brisa knew her sister better than anyone. It was clear they were best friends.

But it was also clear that being Cover Girl to Reyna's Reyna could take a toll.

Wade could see some of the shadow in Brisa's eyes and understood some of the battle Brisa faced.

"We should give her one," Wade murmured. Then he snapped his eyes away from Brisa's. He'd been staring at her for too long. Creepy, right? "Anybody got any suggestions?"

"I told Cookie on my first visit that Queen was my Air Force call sign, because of the meaning of my name. That's the only nickname I've ever had." Reyna grimaced. "Cookie refused to call another woman Queen and was offended by the suggestion, so…"

"Shouldn't be so hard to come up with another one," Sean said, as if he'd already given it some consideration and failed. His glare across the table at Wade was another clue that the nickname had been an issue before, and he didn't appreciate Wade bringing it back up.

Silence settled over their small oasis in the noisy room.

Sean frowned as he concentrated on the wood grain on the table.

Brisa had propped her chin on her hand as she thought.

Wade was sorry he'd made the suggestion. It was supposed to get things back on track, not bring conversation to an abrupt halt. If he had a superpower, that was it: halting normal social interaction in its tracks without even trying.

"What's all the serious about?" Cookie shouted as she slammed two surf plates on the table. Everyone immediately shifted as two more plates loaded with shrimp, scallops, what looked like catfish, hush puppies and a mound of french fries slid across in front of them. "This oughta cheer you up." She motioned the woman standing behind her forward, so that she could wedge in containers of some kind of red sauce, tartar sauce and ketchup. A third server topped off their tea.

It was an organized blitz on the table, executed with precision and speed.

Cookie might have a career in the military if Surf and Turf ever closed.

"Anything else I can get you?" Cookie

asked but she was already moving away. She knew the answer had to be no.

Brisa ripped off paper towels from the holder on the table and handed everyone some. "No napkins. No silverware. Cookie doesn't waste money on the nonessentials." She raised an eyebrow at Wade to gauge his reaction. "You aren't going to make us look bad, are you, Wade?" She picked up a fry and plopped it in her mouth to chew.

Wade shook his head. When in Rome, he could eat with his fingers, too.

And the food was good. Too good to waste time making polite conversation. All four of them focused on their plates until the full platters had been destroyed, although no one cleared their whole meal. The draw to Surf and Turf was clear. Surly service. Lack of amenities. Dangerous ambience.

All wiped away by the power of fried food.

"Somebody mark the calendar. We can't come back for a full month," Brisa said as she collapsed against the booth. "Our arteries will need time to clear."

Wade almost fell for the trap. When people made incorrect medical statements, he often corrected them. Arteries wouldn't magically clear any buildup in a month's time. Then he realized it was conversation, not a diagnosis. No one was in any danger of falling under Brisa's bad medical advice.

"Good thing I'm running in the morning." Sean thumped his stomach. "Mira will not take fried-food hangover as an excuse." His face brightened. "Hey, you could be her new victim. Do you run, Wade?"

Wade balled his paper towel up and put it on the french fry graveyard of his plate. "Treadmill only. I have a nice, air-conditioned gym for that."

Reyna nodded her approval and Brisa laughed at Sean's disappointed expression.

"I knew you were a smart guy, Wade," Reyna said as she shot a glance at her sister and then leaned forward to rest her elbow on the table. "Tell me, if you were looking for a date, what kind of woman would you like to meet?"

It took a second for her words to penetrate his happy food fog. Then he turned to Brisa, who was shaking her head wildly. "I don't know. I didn't…" She huffed out a frustrated sigh. "She was guessing who had asked to be set up, and we just confirmed it was you." Brisa glared at her sister, who had a smug expression on her face. "She was snooping in my phone, found some notifications from the dating website and started asking questions. I hoped it was over, but no."

Reyna patted her sister's hand across the table. "BB, don't worry. Just because I can't tell a lie, doesn't mean I can't figure out when there's more truth behind the crumbs you toss me, especially when I know it's going to be juicy." Then she faced Wade. "Ignore them. Tell me what's going on."

Wade started to answer, but Brisa interrupted. "Wade mentioned he was ready to start dating in Miami, and that he'd love to have some help from a local. You know I love matchmaking, so I volunteered." She shot a "don't you dare say anything else" glare at Wade, so he nodded.

"I've already got the perfect candidate, so there's no need to interrogate the man here in the noise of Surf and Turf." Brisa straightened and motioned Wade to slide out of the booth. "Wade and I have lots of things to take care of at home, so let's get the show moving."

Wade was happy to follow her direction, but Reyna held up a hand.

It was the universal sign to halt.

So Wade stopped sliding.

"Oh, man," Sean muttered under his breath, "just when the two of you were getting along so well, too."

Wade had no clue what that meant, but the other man was shooting him apologetic looks.

"You're about to get caught up in some payback, man. Once upon a time, Reyna was trying to keep a secret about her dream to join the fire department, and Brisa tortured it out of her. Slowly." Sean pressed a hand to the center of his chest. "Do you have any sisters?"

Wade shook his head. "Foster sisters, but we aren't close."

He waited while everyone absorbed that. Eventually, Sean said, "Sisters don't forgive and forget, you know? They remember, and when you think you're safe, boom. They get even. I'd save you from their upcoming battle if I could, but let me say, it's a roller coaster when they argue. Exciting to watch, but if you get stuck on the ride, you might lose your dinner."

Both women turned to glare at Sean, and he held up his hands in surrender. "I'm neutral like Switzerland. Proceed."

"There's no other truth there, Reyna." Brisa motioned at Wade. "Ask him if I'm lying."

Wade wanted to tug on his necktie when the women focused on him, but it was too loose already. He cleared his throat. "Happened just like that. Besides, it's already done. Brisa asked me to come in to talk with her on Monday because she's got a blind date already lined up."

Brisa nodded firmly. Reyna studied her sister, her eyes narrowed as she calculated whatever was happening inside her brain. "With all that's going on at Concord Court and moving and trying to get funding for the business lab and dealing with Luis Montero, you've actually had time to focus on finding a great woman for Wade? You're also still getting lots of dings through the dating app." She scooted back in her seat and crossed her arms over her chest. "I don't buy it."

Since Brisa had done most of her first round of searching for him before everything at Concord Court changed, Wade knew that Reyna was at least half-right. Brisa had a full plate, without his request. Was she one hundred percent correct? Had Brisa lied to him?

Again?

CHAPTER TEN

BRISA HAD BEEN in this same spot often, the one where she wished she could go back in time and just…not do something she'd been convinced had been the right thing in a moment of misguided desire to help.

There were any number of examples. Promising to fund a friend's art show using her father's credit card had been a terrible idea. Making good on her promise had sent her father into the stratosphere. Trusting said "friend" to keep her word about repayment had been the biggest mistake, though. It took Brisa forever to pay back her dad.

Trying to find her sister a handsome date to keep their father's nose out of Reyna's business would have been easy to recover from…

If she'd ever gotten her sister's permission.

But she hadn't. And so far, Wade was going along with her version of events. She might still make it out of this booth at Surf and Turf without her sister yelling.

Or worse, being so disappointed in Brisa.

All she had to do was tell a convincing lie.

Only one thing stopped her. Wade's eyes.

Telling the truth now was going to hurt. Lying to him again and being found out at some point in the future would be worse. Already, he'd transitioned from nice enough acquaintance to a good guy who had a whole personality and a list of dreams for his life, too. Someone like a friend. Experiencing Surf and Turf together probably had a way of bonding people like that.

"I haven't actually settled on the person yet, but there are a couple of good options for Wade to choose from." There. A pinch of truth with enough vagueness to get herself out of trouble. Maybe.

Nobody was buying it. Wade's expression changed. It was impossible to describe how, but the warmth of friendship founded on fried food faded. He grew cooler.

Reyna did what she had always done, over a lifetime of big sistering. She stepped in to save Brisa. "Good. Great. That means we still have time to fine-tune the decision." She smiled broadly at Wade. "Tell me what you're looking for. I'm really good at this.

"Pretty, of course. Late thirties." Reyna tapped the table. "What else is important?" She wasn't writing a list, but Brisa was certain her sister was flipping through her mental catalog of single women she knew.

Wade cleared his throat. "Military. Likes kids because Thea is the most important person to me. Okay with the demands of my career."

Reyna pursed her lips. "Why military?"

Annoyed at her sister again, Brisa was determined to get the evening over with as fast as possible. She wrapped her hand around Wade's arm and tried to nudge him out of the booth again. "Because Wade, like you, like at least half of the veterans I talk to, thinks that only another veteran can understand what he or she's been through. They don't want to talk any more about their experience than they have to. They're absolutely certain that military scars are completely different from the types of wounds all the rest of us carry. And in some cases, that may be true, but the fact is, bad things happen every day to civilians, too, unfortunately. Any of this sound familiar, Reyna? Stop badgering the witness."

Reyna covered her heart with her hands. "I never said that, did I? I don't think my scars are that much different than a lot of other people's." She frowned as she considered the question.

"I'm pretty sure I said it. I know Jason Ward had to be persuaded to drop that kind of thinking when he was trying to talk himself out of liking the professor." Sean's expression was serious. "I get it."

"Reyna, you're you," Brisa said and waved her hand generally. "Capable of handling it all by yourself. Not everyone is that way."

"That isn't true, Brisa. People who don't know her might say that, but we know her." Sean wrapped an arm around Reyna, always their peacemaker.

Since Wade hadn't spoken, Brisa wasn't sure which way he was taking the conversation. "You're right. It's just…" She sighed. "The only woman I can think of who would be right for Wade is already in love with one of my best friends."

Watching Sean's slow smile was sweet until he realized fully what she was saying.

"Someone like Reyna who is not Reyna," he muttered and frowned at Wade.

Wade held both hands up in surrender. Whatever Sean was figuring out, he hadn't gotten to the catfishing truth yet and Brisa refused to escort him the rest of the way.

"Hand me your phone. We can flip through the choices and talk them over." Reyna held out her hand.

When Reyna used the "bossy big sis" tone, Brisa usually had one of two reactions. The easiest was compliance. She liked the easy way, but not tonight. When Wade wrapped his hand around hers under the table, she jolted and turned his direction. Some of the warmth had returned.

Before she could straighten her spine and object to Reyna, Wade said, "I'm happy with the setup. Brisa understands what I want."

Reyna's eyebrows shot up, so Brisa braced herself for...something. She wasn't sure what her older sister might say in the face of having her orders ignored.

Reyna nodded. "Okay, good enough for me, then." She pointed at the plates on the table. "Everyone's finished. Should we go?"

Relieved, Brisa jostled to get out of the booth. "Yeah, yeah. Wade has been dying to check out the observation point. Meet us outside."

"That's our cue to give them some privacy, dear." Sean grabbed the bill and pulled Reyna out behind him to weave through the tables.

Wade didn't follow. Instead, he stared at her solemnly. Whatever commotion there was around them, he and Brisa might have been caught in a bubble of privacy. He didn't need words to tell her they weren't through with the conversation about why she'd lied again. She wanted him to know that she understood that and that she had a few words to say to him about the whole thing, too. When they were both clear, he started to walk.

As Brisa followed, she tried to remember the last time she'd been on the same page with a man, so connected that they could communicate, even temporarily resolve problems, without a word. No one came to mind, not even the kid she'd married when she was a kid, too. They'd done all their talking in loud bursts, either excited or angry.

Facing a man who could tell her what was going on inside his head with one stare was new.

And exciting.

When he offered her his hand, she slipped her hand in his easily. Maybe too easily. Wade made it easy.

Something else she was going to have to give some serious thought to later.

As they stepped outside, Reyna and Sean were already pressed close to the wooden railing that circled the highest deck, a perch about fifty feet from the door that continued up to a point farther away. During the day, visitors would see more marsh, mangroves and wide-open space that turned into ocean at some point.

"Surf and Turf comes with dinner and a show," Sean said as he pointed over the side. Wade leaned to look down, way, way down into inky darkness.

Brisa remembered her first visit, also at night. She'd been certain something was watching her from the water below. Sean guffawed at the way she'd shrieked at a noise. Then he'd whimpered at her firm grip on his arm all the way back to the car while Reyna laughed.

"Why do I get the creepy sensation something is watching me?" Wade asked as he took a step back. Brisa's eyebrows shot up in surprise, but she didn't mention they were on the same page.

"I'm not sure gators have that good eyesight, but maybe," Reyna said thoughtfully.

"Restaurants with pet alligators," Wade muttered. "Only in Florida."

"There's a barricade built under the lowest level of the piers," Brisa said softly before she squeezed his hand. "Sean's been here long enough that he's soaked in some Florida Man tendencies, but this is one of those things that separates tourists from the locals. We're safe."

Wade nodded but he didn't let go of her hand. "Does this mean I'm part of the family? Are there any other tests I need to be prepared for?"

The family? That was a sweet way to put it.

"Eating the best seafood on a plate? Some test!" Brisa cleared her throat. A strange lump there was giving her trouble. "You aren't going to put regular visits to Surf and Turf on your calendar, then?"

Wade bent closer. "Only if you're with me. I need to know what to keep an eye out for. If Cookie doesn't get me, the gators might."

When he tangled their fingers together, everything stopped. Brisa wanted to stay there in the shadows, just the two of them, until she understood what was happening between them.

"Are you guys coming?" Reyna shouted from the stairs leading back down to the parking lot.

Brisa tugged him forward. "My sister tempts me to toss her to the gators now and then. I'm glad you were with us tonight. It has been a long day." She closed her eyes. "She's effective, yes, but there's never a minute to rest."

He wrinkled his nose. "We should give Reyna and Thea a project. I don't know who could come out on top, but as long as we stayed far away and watched from a distance, it would be awe-inspiring."

Brisa smiled. "We better catch up. I don't think Sean will leave without us, but Reyna might try giving the order."

"They're good together," he murmured as they went down the steps. "Spending time with them makes me optimistic about dating and jealous enough to ruin my digestion."

"Because you didn't have a chance to get to know Reyna first?" Brisa asked lightly, even though she didn't want the answer.

"No, because I want something like they have, that easy love where they see each other clearly, the good and the not so good, and neither one is worried about losing it. Most people try to hide that stuff. I know I did." Wade pulled her hand through the crook in his elbow, as if they were descending a grand staircase instead of a weathered gator overlook in the middle of nowhere.

Apparently Wade McNally had layers.

"Yeah, neither Reyna nor Sean have to hide much. They're both great." Brisa bit back a sigh. She understood why Wade had mentioned jealousy. "You should go with that 'being yourself' thing, too. You're great, too. Any woman would agree."

All she did was hide things. Her whole life, that had been her way to cope with being out of step wherever she was.

Wade didn't argue, though. It was good advice she'd given.

They were quiet as they maneuvered the rest of the dark stairs back to the parking lot and slid into the car. Reyna and Sean were both quiet, too.

Brisa always enjoyed the drive out to Surf and Turf. She'd grown up in Coral Gables; lived here and there all over the world and spent most of her time in the big, vibrant city of Miami. This place? Might as well have been on a different planet.

The company was always good, though. Brisa had no secrets from Reyna except for Military Match; they could talk about anything.

Sean could be counted on to keep things light and entertaining. Tonight, Wade had drawn some of the attention, too.

Taking her side after Reyna offered to step in to help set him up had been sweet and unexpected. He'd been so upset when he'd cornered her on the rooftop. In his spot tonight, she'd have been dying to spill the beans on whoever had tried to trick her.

Wade had kept his promise. At the same time, he'd given her a vote of confidence, too. Did he understand that? Probably not.

He definitely didn't understand how much that loyalty meant to Brisa.

Sean parked in front of Reyna's unit. "Y'all have a good evening. We're going to take Dottie for her nightly constitutional."

"I'm working the next three days at the station, but you can call me if you need me." Reyna hugged Brisa after they both exited the car. "Not that you will need me," she told Brisa.

Wade and Sean shook hands. "Thanks for dinner. I'll pick up the check next time," Wade said as he stepped up on the sidewalk.

"I'll be sure to pick a more expensive place, then." Sean let out an "oof" even though he managed to catch Reyna's jab before it connected with his abdomen. "And listen, I don't know everything that goes into matchmaking." He bent his head closer and murmured, "But between you and me, I know as much as either one of them." Sean grinned. "You want to meet someone great, slip on your running shoes and meet me at the pool about sunrise."

Brisa exchanged a look with her sister.

"Mira," Sean said. "Pretty. Retired Air Force medic. Must like kids because she's going to be a teacher. Tends to give orders that make men run faster, but that's on purpose because she's our amateur personal trainer. As a man who understands the lure of a woman who is a smidge intimidating," Sean added as he pulled Reyna closer, "I'd say she's perfect for Wade's foray into dating in his new life."

She and Reyna exchanged glances again.

"I've explained that mental telepathy only works for twins and that they are not, in fact, twins, although the attitudes are very similar, but…" Sean shook his head.

"Would Mira be interested in a blind date?" Brisa asked, her hands clutched under her chin. She'd been through all the other options on the website that showed interest in Wade and rejected them.

Dating sites were terrible. She might as well have thrown a dart at a picture.

But Mira… Brisa didn't know her well, but she was a part of the inner circle that hung out at the pool at midnight. All veterans. All in need of the chance to talk with others who understood. Mira might not be a Reyna Montero, but she was an exciting choice.

"Interested in a blind date," Sean repeated slowly. "I'm guessing no."

Reyna opened her mouth to add something. Brisa wasn't sure whether it would be advice or intended for Sean, but he spun her sister around and they both walked away and up the steps to their door.

Brisa could see the blur of a bouncing Dalmatian when the door opened and closed behind them.

She turned back to face Wade. "He's right."

"About which part?" Wade asked. Brisa had unlocked her door and only then noticed he hadn't followed her. Her plan was to keep the evening going, even though she was worn-out. For some reason, she'd have been happy to talk to him longer. He'd had a big day, too. Was he waiting for her to get inside safely? Sweet.

Brisa crossed her arms over her chest. "Sean's right about all of it. Do not tell him I said that. Mira would be a great woman to introduce you to. She may not be looking for you, but I do have some solid powers of persuasion. When you come in on Monday, I'll have the details worked out. Trust me."

Wade shoved his hands in his pockets. "I trusted you last time and you were... not telling the truth. What's different this time?" There was no anger in his expression, but it was harder to see his eyes given where he stood on the shadowy sidewalk.

What an excellent question. She'd known him less than a week and already let him down how many times? Why would he trust her?

But that question reminded her of her father's stern face while they'd met in her office about what to do with Concord Court.

What a moment to come to grips with her own part in the mess of her family's drama. Using half-truths to smooth everything over made big messes. Always had. When was she going to try something different?

She huffed out a heavy breath. "Here's the thing. My intentions are always good. They are. But I overpromise and under-deliver. Over thirty-plus years. It's time to get a grip on that. You deserve the truth." She marched back down the steps. "I'm going to talk to Mira and do my absolute best to convince her this is an excellent opportunity because it is. I'll do that by the time I close the office on Monday. If I can't convince her, I'll keep looking." She held out her hand. "Shake my hand. It almost killed me to hedge my bets that way."

He chuckled as he shook her hand. "Why? It was nearly the way almost everyone makes promises."

Another good question. "I know what you want. I like you. I want you to have it. That's the key to every bad decision I've made over a lifetime." She seesawed her head. "To be fair, all of the good ones, too."

Wade finally nodded. "Fair enough. I'd rather have that, Brisa, the truth."

"Even when it's not what you want to hear?" Brisa asked.

Wade stared hard at the sidewalk. "Yeah. Even then."

"Okay," Brisa said. She'd have to see how this played out.

Before he could go, she leaned forward and wrapped her arms around his neck. His hesitation had the awkward flush spreading on her face, but then he wrapped his arms around her and held her. The hug went from a thank-you to genuine comfort in an instant.

"What's this for?" he asked, his voice husky in her ear. The vibration stole her breath and sent a small shiver down her back.

"You didn't tell Reyna what I did. It must have been tempting to make an example of my bad behavior. And you chose my help over hers." Brisa didn't meet his eyes as she said it but tried to make a joke. "No one else in the world would do that."

When she would have stepped back, Wade held her close. She wasn't sure how long they stood there. Eventually he said, "You can trust me, Brisa. I'll never tell the story of why we met. And over dinner tonight, I realized how lucky I was that Reyna found Sean before I showed up. She's not the one for me." He eased back. "Thanks for saving me from the gators. Introduce me to Reggie the next time he's around, okay?"

She nodded.

Then she realized he'd stand there on the sidewalk until she was safely inside.

"Good night," Brisa said softly and fumbled with the doorknob until she got the door open. After she stepped inside, she locked the door and collapsed against it.

Had she ever enjoyed a night out in jeans and a T-shirt like she had this one?

No.

At that point, it was difficult to remember any other night, any other conversation, any other man's arms around her that she'd enjoyed more.

If she thought about it, it made perfect sense for her messed-up world.

One man she was feeling all these new things for, emotions she couldn't name because they were unfamiliar...and she was supposed to find him the perfect woman to fall in love with.

Another classic Brisa Montero mess.

CHAPTER ELEVEN

ON SATURDAY MORNING, after a truly sleep-less night, Brisa made a decision she would regret for days. She put on her like-new jogging shoes and waited next to the pool for Mira's sunrise running group.

Somehow, she was the first one there.

That was no mystery. Given her long night, she was relieved to see the morning start. For hours, Brisa had alternated between two terrible choices.

First, she could clench her eyes closed in an effort to will herself to sleep so that she'd stop thinking about Wade McNally and the chaos she was making with him that could ruin their relationship and result in her making a colossal disaster of Concord Court by failing on the small business lab and the twisty road that had gotten her there.

Or, second, she could stare blearily at the

thick binders she now carried with her at all times like the world's most boring security blanket. She'd successfully made two notes in the very early morning. Replaying Wade's every word and expression the previous night reminded her she wanted to get a best benefits guide or retirement planner for folks at Concord Court, to provide them guidance with the decisions Wade had mentioned he'd struggled over. The other note, regarding addiction counselors or support groups, needed more input.

Where did she hope to get that input? All roads turned right back to Wade in an annoying loop.

Running could be a gift, a completely different loop with actual scenery.

"Wow, I did not expect this," Mira said as she approached through the courtyard. "I'm always the first one here and you're never here." She gathered her long dark hair in a sloppy ponytail and braced her hands on her hips. "To what do I owe this?"

Was this the right time? Brisa hesitated to make her request before she'd had any room to lay the groundwork. Convincing people to go her way was usually something she spent careful hours plotting. This? Her decision to go running had been spontaneous.

Then she remembered her promise to herself to spend more time with the truth.

"Long night. I couldn't sleep. I thought this would help with some of the anxiety." All of that was true, even if it wasn't the whole truth. "Please don't make me regret it." She smiled at Mira to help her understand it was a friendly request. "I run, but I'm not a road warrior like your group."

Mira snorted. "Have you actually met Sean Wakefield? I could have run circles around him when I was in elementary school at field day. You don't have anything to worry about. If you hit your limit, peel off and head back home. Everyone starts at different levels, and they're all good as far as I'm concerned." Her smile seemed genuine when she added, "I'm grateful to have another woman on the run. The belly-aching from the men can be a lot to handle without someone along who understands how I enjoy their complaints."

Before Brisa had to come up with any other conversation, Sean and Marcus Bryant, the quiet landscaper who'd been her back-bone for the small business lab she desperately wanted to get off the ground, walked up.

"You didn't mention you'd be here this morning," Sean said as he wrapped an arm around her shoulders and yanked her closer for a hard hug and an annoying scrub of his hand through her neat ponytail. Amusement was in his eyes when he asked in an innocent tone, "What brought this on?"

He knew very well what brought it on: his suggestion that Mira was the right date for Wade, and Brisa's need to get herself out of this latest predicament by somehow convincing Mira to give it a shot.

"Talk later," Mira said as Peter Kim and Jason Ward appeared. Both acknowledged Brisa by rolling their eyes at Mira's order. "Brisa, you fall in behind me. Sean behind Brisa. Keep an eye on her and when she turns back, you go with her. The rest of you…just fall in."

Muttering filled the air, but Mira was already gone, and Brisa had to hustle to get in line.

After the first mile, Brisa realized she

hadn't spent enough time thinking this plan through. She wanted to complete the run, but her fitness level was "jogging at the gym while she read books on her phone," and this group's? Yeah, it was about years spent carrying gear, dodging drill instructors and staying alive. The two did not mesh.

But after the third mile, something happened. All the voices shouting that she was going to die if she didn't stop and catch her breath faded. She picked up the rhythm of the run, her feet falling steadily and smoothly on the pavement, while her breathing deepened and her heart rate strengthened and panic dropped away. Brisa didn't have to do anything except put one foot in front of the other and keep pace with Mira.

She'd expected to remember scenery, but it was all a blur.

Mira's slowed pace was still a gift when they turned back into the driveway of Concord Court.

When Sean collapsed to sit on the curb in front of the office, Brisa did the same. Mira paced in a tight line in front of them, while the rest of the guys didn't even slow down. They might have picked up the pace as they headed for their showers.

"You did good, Montero," Mira said. "Six miles on your first run. I didn't expect that."

Brisa hadn't, either, and learning she'd run six miles immediately made every single inch of her body cry out in pain. "Good. I'm glad. If you'll get a shovel and bury me here, I'd appreciate it." Then she stretched out on the warm sidewalk and closed her eyes. What had she been thinking?

Sean tried to laugh but it was more like a wheeze. "You were supposed to stop sooner, Brisa. Then I was going to get early relief, too, but no, you had to keep running." He mirrored her response by stretching out. "Bury us both here. Tell Reyna to go on with her life."

Mira shook her head. "You're both going to have to recover. I do not want Reyna Montero coming after me for killing her boyfriend and her sister, even though you volunteered for this. She's never made this morning run with us, so I don't know if I can outrun her or not." Mira held out both hands and tugged them back to their feet.

Sean stepped up on the sidewalk. "I've got to open up the office, or my boss might fire me. You two have a nice day." His eyes met Brisa's before he turned to go. She was going to take it as encouragement to continue with her plan to make her case to Mira.

The fabled endorphin rush from exercise might make Mira susceptible.

"When he makes himself curiously absent, I know something is up. Sean Wakefield would rather yammer in my ear about how mean I am than leave quietly." Mira tapped her chin. "Why am I sure this is not a coincidence with your unexpected presence?"

Brisa knew she'd never get a better opening, but for some reason, she hesitated.

Mira met all the criteria. And no one had ever had a bad word to say about her. She was even the heart of the unofficial therapy group that met most nights around the pool. Wade would like her, too.

Was that the issue? She didn't want Wade to like Mira? Liking wasn't the problem.

Falling in love might be, but Brisa couldn't answer why the image of the two of them in love bothered her.

"Hello?" Mira waved a hand in front of Brisa's face. "Anyone home?"

Brisa blinked and shook her head. "Sorry. I was having a long conversation in my head, one side of me arguing with the other. Weird, right?"

Mira drawled, "Girl, if I had a dollar for every time I've done the same…"

"Okay," Brisa said firmly, "I did want to talk to you about something, an exciting opportunity."

Mira frowned. "I'm not buying time-shares or a condo in Fort Lauderdale. Wrong audience. I'm about to start my first year as a public-school teacher, broke but fulfilled."

"Better opportunity than some time-share, and there's no money required." Brisa motioned toward a shady table by the wrought-iron fence that wrapped the pool. Every time she walked through the ornate gates, Brisa remembered how her father had hit the roof of his high-rise office over the price tag.

It had still been the right decision. Everyone who visited remarked on this pool. It was a selling point. An oasis from the hustle and bustle, and worse. That certainty boosted her slipping confidence.

When Mira propped her elbows on the arms of the chair and huffed out a breath, Brisa realized she was losing momentum. "I don't know what your dating situation is, but there's someone I'd like to set you up with. He's great, a veteran like you, distinguished military career and a doctor."

Mira blinked slowly at her. Brisa was on the verge of waving her own hand in Mira's face when she shook her head. "A blind date? That's your amazing opportunity? Do people even do that anymore?"

"Handsome. Smart. Successful. A guy like this is rarer than an affordable timeshare," Brisa said as she leaned forward. "He's a surgeon. You were a medic, right? Love science? He's got the cutest daughter, nine years old, who dreams of visiting outer space." Was it a mistake including Thea? Brisa bit her lip as she watched Mira. Then she realized it would have been a huge misstep not to mention Wade's daughter. Thea was his world. Everyone should find that as attractive as Brisa did.

Mira turned to stare at the clear pool, so Brisa did the same. The day was going to be hot. The water was already tempting. The urge to escape the conversation, to take a running leap and land with a splash, was strong. She wasn't sure her tightening muscles would comply.

"I've got no interest in dating, not even this rare specimen you've discovered." Mira made the "give it to me" motion with her hand. "Hit me with it. If he's so great, why aren't you scooping him up for yourself?"

The man had had his heart set on Reyna. No way would Brisa even provide a close substitute.

Brisa jerked as she realized how bothered she was by that answer. She was fulfilling a promise and keeping herself out of trouble. Nothing more. Right?

"I have a boyfriend. Otherwise I'd…" Brisa left the option dangling as she remembered Reggie. He was more a prop than a boyfriend, and she was less satisfied with that setup this morning than she ever had been before, but it worked for her in this moment, so she went with it. "I'll get you reservations at the nicest restaurant in Miami. Rooftop. View of the city. You can put on a beautiful dress and enjoy a great meal. What do you have to lose?"

Mira raised an eyebrow. "All the money it would take to find a wardrobe and stylist for something like that." She grimaced. "Not my scene."

Brisa tangled her fingers together in her lap. That had been a mistake. The fact that it was the only kind of date she and Reggie ever managed made it easy to imagine, but it wasn't tempting.

"Of course not. You're right. How about…" Brisa closed her eyes as she tried to come up with something unique, something that might draw Mira out.

The last time she'd modeled for one of the boutiques in the Design District, the shoot had been in Wynwood, home of galleries, street art and artists. They'd had to pack up and move locations because tours kept interrupting the shoot. Would Mira enjoy something like that? If so, Brisa could call in a favor. "How about a bicycle tour through Wynwood? I'll get an artist to be your guide, you can ask questions, and the conversation will be easy. No new wardrobe required, either."

Mira studied her face as she considered the offer. "I have wanted to do more exploring before I start to work. I've been so focused on school and spending time with my family that..." She held up a finger. "On one condition, I'll say yes."

Brisa fought to contain her relief and said, "I'm listening."

"I like running with another woman in the group, two reasonable heads instead of one." Mira's lips slowly curled into a grin. "Join my running group."

Since Brisa was still nearly certain her muscles had formed a revolutionary party of their own and would punish her for the morning at some point, she hesitated.

But her pride at managing the run hadn't faded.

Mira held both arms out as if she was prepared for whatever Brisa could throw at her. "Do we have a deal? I'll date your bachelor once. I will not date any other bachelors you bring forth in any shape or fashion. In exchange, you help me keep the guys running. Everyone wins."

Brisa had negotiated so many similar situations lately. The loophole that needed to be closed was big. Setting a time frame only made sense. Instead of firmly establishing an expiration date on her running experiment, say for a month or a week or whatever she could get Mira to agree to, she nodded. "It's a deal. I'll text you the time and a meeting place for this date. Is next Saturday okay?"

"Sure." Mira stood. Brisa followed and managed to bite back the whimper that boiled up from the tightness in her calves. "You should stretch. Take a warm shower. Tomorrow, cut the run in half." She smoothed loose hair off her forehead. "Sean will thank you."

Brisa nodded. "If I can walk tomorrow, I'll meet you here." She might still be sitting in this chair if her legs refused to carry her home anyway.

"If you don't meet me here, I'll come searching for you." Mira pointed at her. "You should have negotiated harder." Then she waved and left through the opposite gate. Brisa watched her trot away and wondered why she hadn't tried harder to get better terms.

Then she realized she wanted Mira to like her. Managing to keep up with the run had been about proving herself to Mira as well as to herself that she could do it. Being coerced into joining the run officially was a confirmation that she'd done exactly that, proven herself.

And it felt good.

Making good on her promise to line up an exciting date for Wade was the cherry on top. All in all, it had been a successful morning.

If she could make it back to her townhome, she'd take a shower and a nap in that order. There would be time to celebrate her success and figure out why it didn't feel better later.

CHAPTER TWELVE

WHEN WADE USHERED his daughter inside the Concord Court office on Monday afternoon, he could tell they'd come at exactly the wrong time. Thea led the way, excited to meet Dottie again. At first glance, he wasn't sure if the situation required ambulance, fire and police response or if it was run-of-the-mill "must be a Monday" bad. Brisa was crying. That caught his attention. Sean hovered nearby with a phone in one hand, held carefully to Brisa's ear, and a bottle of water in the other.

Brisa saw them enter first. She immediately wiped under both eyes and waved her hands at Sean. He checked over his shoulder and then put the phone up to his own ear. "Reyna, gotta go. I'll call you back." He listened. "Someone's come into the office. Brisa's got it under control. Stay where you are for the rest of your shift at the station unless I call for help." The call ended and he slipped the phone into his pocket. "Miss Thea McNally, we finally meet."

Sean offered a warm smile. Thea's giggle lightened some of the tension in the room. "How do you know who I am?"

Wade had told more than one story about Thea at Surf and Turf, but Sean said, "Brisa mentioned your exquisite design sense, Milky Way–themed. That's my favorite candy bar!" He tapped Thea's inflatable ring, dark blue and patterned with shooting stars, of course. Thea had insisted on blowing it up and stepping into it so that it completed her swimming ensemble before the door had closed on his townhome. It was time to cross "pool" off her important daily agenda and nothing was going to slow her down. "This is worthy of a future astronaut."

Wade watched various emotions march across his daughter's face. She was enchanted by Sean Wakefield immediately. The guy probably had that effect on most women.

It seemed she also desperately wanted to correct him. "The Milky Way is a galaxy, the home of our solar system." Thea frowned. "You know that, right?"

"Really?" Sean asked, his face a comical mask of curiosity. "Come help me skim the pool and tell me more." He met Wade's stare, a silent check to make sure Wade was okay with that. Wade gave Sean a nearly invisible nod.

Thea picked up the conversation as she and Sean went back outside. Wade watched them for a second as Sean picked up the long pool skimmer and demonstrated the proper form for getting bugs out of the water. Thea studied the technique carefully and then bent over with a belly laugh. Wade had no idea what Sean was saying, but his daughter was okay for the moment.

He turned back to Brisa. She immediately dropped the compact she'd been using to straighten up her mascara into a desk drawer and slammed it shut. "Wade. How is the move coming along?" Her tone was brisk. Professional. He hated it.

"Good." He crossed his arms over his chest and swayed from watching Thea out the window to trying to meet Brisa's cool smile. "It's Monday, so…" He no longer wanted to talk about a date. Finding out what was wrong mattered more, but how to get the information he wanted without upsetting her again…

Brisa inhaled slowly and let it go. "Yes, it is, and the next step in your dating future is something I actually accomplished." She closed the binder on her desk with a thud and straightened her shoulders. "When you're on a downhill slide, it's important to celebrate the wins. You and Mira have a date on Saturday. She's excited to meet you. You'll both have a good time."

Wade moved closer to the desk. Her tone was hard to read. He wanted to see her eyes. As he sat down across from her, she blinked rapidly. The urge to hand her a tissue or a drink or something to keep those tears away was hard to fight.

Brisa said, "I shouldn't say that. I have no clue if you'll like her or if she'll want to get to know you. *Excited* isn't the right word for her attitude, either, but she did agree." Her shoulders slumped. "I'm doing it again. Making promises that people want and that I have no way of carrying out.

When will I learn?" She covered her face with her hands.

The threat of more tears shimmered in the air of the office. Some women were messy criers, but Brisa managed to seem tragic and beautiful at the same time. Wade wanted to get rid of the tragedy. He only knew one way to handle that: solve the problem.

First, he had to figure out what the problem was.

To do that, he had to keep her talking.

"Do you have a recommendation for a restaurant? If you can help with that, you're off the hook. You've made good on your promise." Watching her struggle to keep a pleasant expression on her face was painful. At this point, he wanted to do anything he could to chase the tears away.

"Even better," Brisa said as she slid a paper across the desk. She sniffed once. "Mira wanted to do anything but fancy dinner with a city view, so I booked you two into a tour of Wynwood."

Wade frowned as he picked up the paper. What was Wynwood and why did it have tours? "On bicycles?" Wade asked aloud.

Brisa's smile faded and she clamped her hands to her forehead. "You don't know how to ride a bike. Oh, no."

Wade stretched to wrap a hand around her wrist. He pulled it across the desk and held firmly. Smooth, warm skin over delicate bones, something he'd always remember. "I know how to ride a bike. What kind of tour is this?"

She stared at his hand on her arm for too long before she looked up. Wade forced himself to lean back.

"Wynwood is this Miami neighborhood with lots of murals, graffiti, artists with funky studios. This tour will take you through the area with an artist as a guide. You can get some history, some personal stories, plenty of time for you and Mira to talk about whatever comes up, and if it goes well, there are cafés where you can grab a drink." Brisa wrinkled her nose. "Not a fan of art?"

Wade shook his head. "Not a fan of galleries, but this could be…fun." He smiled at the way she punched one fist in the air. "And with a set tour, we'll have an easy excuse to call it quits when it's over. You might have a knack for this after all."

Brisa brushed off both shoulders. "I'll keep trying. Eventually, I'll find something I have a real talent for." She tried to make the joke, but her smile wobbled on the edges. "I'm not sure it's a great sign that you're both looking for an early ending, but I told Mira you'd meet her there." She texted him the time and place for the tour. "No unnecessary pressure for either of you."

Wade nodded. "Hmm, so Mira needed convincing that we're perfect for each other." Over the weekend, he'd started to have some doubts that he was on the right track himself. Why else would Brisa be the only woman on his mind? Even the memory of her kiss with Reggie Beaumont had failed to chase away the thoughts for long.

"Mira hasn't met you yet. But she'll be excited for a second date. You can count on it." Brisa patted his hand—the consolation prize a beautiful woman might give her kindly old grandfather.

On that note, Wade decided he'd left

his daughter in the care of Sean for long enough.

Or maybe it was vice versa.

"I hope tomorrow is better for you," Wade said as he paused at the door. "I won't push, but if I can help with…anything, please let me know."

Brisa's lips flattened. "It has to be. I got not one but two rejections to grant proposals I was counting on. They said my requests didn't meet the criteria, but I know they did. I failed to present them correctly. That's the only answer I can come up with. I'm glad I found out after meeting with my father this morning. I have a week to find a solution. I built the budget I pitched on those grants and…" She covered her face again. "You should go. I can't keep the tears away forever."

Since he knew next to nothing about grants, Wade couldn't come up with any words of advice. Why was he stuck in the doorway? He didn't want to leave her like this.

"Oh, before you go," Brisa said with a frown as she dug around her desk and pulled out a different binder than the one causing her such distress, "I wanted to get your opinion on something." She ran a finger down the open page. "Jason Ward works here part-time as a job coach who helps with résumés, interview skills, that kind of thing. He's going to make some calls this week to track down a benefits adviser who would be willing to volunteer time to help us with seminars, retirement planning, that kind of thing. Most of the veterans who come through here will be like you, with a collection of military benefits and first-time options available through new employers, or they may be the ones able to offer them via their businesses."

Wade rested his shoulder against the wall. "Okay. Why do you need my opinion on that?" He was not the right guy to be offering expertise. The decisions he had to make still caused a knot in his stomach when he remembered to worry about them. Considering a call to Whitney in HR for anything other than retirement advice made it worse. Whitney? Was that her name? He hoped he'd written it down somewhere.

Brisa finally glanced up from her notebook. "Oh, that's not what I need your input on. I was passing along the info in case you needed it. He'll give you a call as soon as we've found the right adviser."

Wade nodded slowly. He'd play along. It was distracting her from tears. Watching her certainty and confidence peek through was magnetic.

Brisa shrugged. "Friday night. At Surf and Turf. After your orientation at the hospital?" She rolled her hands to encourage him to catch up. "When Cookie called you 401(k), I realized there were going to be other men and women like you who could use some help navigating all their options. Have you forgotten? You were at the end of your rope."

Wade banged his head softly against the wall. "I have a month to figure it all out. I decided not to think about it until then. Too many decisions and I can't..." Focus. That was his problem, he'd decided. In a world of options, his chances of making a bad choice were too high. For years, his options had been narrow. Easy to evaluate.

He'd made one throwaway remark about

something that was a minor thing in the overall scheme of life at Concord Court.

Brisa had already worked up a solution. He was impressed.

"Here's my opinion. Good job." Wade straightened up as he watched her face brighten. Brisa didn't immediately answer, and Wade realized she was studying him. He'd dressed for the pool, trunks and a T-shirt. Her eyes had done the full sweep. Was she checking him out?

There were several seconds of an awkward silence before she cleared her throat and said, "I'm sorry. I just realized you were heading out to swim and I'm holding you up." Then she shook her head. "I still don't have the input I wanted." She tapped the binder. "After Surf and Turf, I made two notes. The benefits counselor and..." Brisa bit her lip. Whatever it was, she hesitated to ask. Since she'd gone pretty bravely after all sorts of things, he was curious. Wade stepped closer.

"I assume your sobriety has come with the help of a program, one of the anonymous twelve-step groups?" She bent the corner of the page in front of her, frowned and then smoothed it out again. "Should I try to start up something similar here or would it be better to have information on local existing groups included in the welcome packet?" She cleared her throat again. "What I guess I'm asking is how important is the anonymity piece?"

Wade scratched his chin as he considered her question and the discomfort she was showing in asking it. Brisa cared enough to want to help. Even more important, she wanted to help in the best way for the people who needed it, not the easiest way or the way that would get good press.

"Okay, that's a bigger question." He propped his hands on his hips, watched how her eyes followed the action and enjoyed the lift in his spirit since he was certain she was checking him out. He was *never* certain when a woman was checking him out. For it to be Brisa, that made him invincible. "For me, there was no hiding my problem. Nearly destroyed my career." He hated that her eyes snapped to his face. Whatever she'd thought of him before, he'd sink in her estimation now. "A nurse anesthetist watched me stagger into my office and that was pretty much all it had taken. I was barred from surgery until there was an evaluation. She kept me from making a mistake that might have destroyed another person's life and my whole world. Part of the requirements I had to meet to keep my job was mandatory attendance every week to a support group for alcoholics. My problem and my only option to keep my job weren't secrets for long." He grimaced. "It was an experience, hitting rock bottom and swimming around down there with the others trying to climb out, but that group made all the difference. Couldn't save my marriage, but it saved everything else. So…" He studied Brisa's face. The tears were gone, but she was still sadder than he liked. "My opinion is that there are already groups doing the work. It would be better to have the information on the variety of resources available than to build something here. I think. Anonymity wasn't really a part of my recovery, but I don't want anyone to miss out on the opportunity because they need to meet with people and can't be exposed to the whole world. I think."

She'd wanted his honest opinion and he'd given it.

Brisa relaxed in her chair. "I like that answer. So much. I'm going to take that to the therapist and the professor of social work at Sawgrass University who we liaise with, but I wanted your input first. So, thank you."

That was easy. Wade didn't want to make decisions for others. He had enough trouble with his own, but it mattered that Brisa valued his opinion for some reason. He wanted her to value him.

He realized that Brisa wasn't judging him as broken beyond repair, even after he'd told her the worst memory he had. His record of service and expertise had earned him a second chance after a suspension, rehab and ongoing group therapy. There wouldn't be a third one. That was enough to prevent the craving that sometimes showed up from overwhelming him. His life had no room for the mistakes alcohol would cause.

If he ever remarried, he wanted someone who could accept his truth and make him stronger. It was a lot to ask of anyone.

"I should go save Sean. If you'd like to do some swimming, Thea McNally will be providing the entertainment for the next hour or so." Wade motioned over his shoulder. "Join us if you'd like. It will take your mind off everything else. Trust me, you will have no time to focus on anything except Thea."

Brisa pointed at the clock. "Office closed five minutes ago. I might do that."

The jolt of excitement that energized him made no sense. Was this a friendship? Something else? Meeting Brisa at the pool was meaningless fun, that was all. Wade's internal monologue on that theme was stern as he walked out to the pool.

He had a date with another woman for Saturday.

Why hadn't the promise of that sparked anything but dread?

Wade joined in with the swimmers. "Everything okay?" Sean asked. He was dangling his legs in the cold water next to Wade, while Thea floated in lazy circles on her back. "You're smiling. That has to be a good sign." Sean turned to wave at Brisa.

"I forwarded the phones to the emergency number and locked up," she called as she hurried past them. "Office is closed for the day, Sean. You're officially off duty."

Sean saluted. "Will do. I'm going to meet Reyna and Dottie at the fire station for dinner. Any words you want me to pass along?" He stood and kicked his feet to dry off. "She worries, you know."

"If you wouldn't call her ten times a day, she wouldn't know enough to worry, Sean." Brisa rolled her eyes.

"She'd know. She's got some kind of sixth sense for her baby sister. You gonna be okay?" Sean asked. Wade watched Brisa tip her chin up. He'd seen Reyna do the same at the cocktail party on the hotel rooftop. Both Montero sisters had steel spines, even if it looked different on Reyna.

"I will be. There are other grants, other days, and I'll figure this out." Then she nodded and strode away.

Sean sighed. "One minute, Reyna and Brisa seem like they're going to kill each other. The next, they're challenging any oncomers who would dare say a word against one of them." He grinned at Wade. "Falling for a Montero sister is an adventure. I'd tell you not to do it, but I'd be wasting my time." Then he raised an eyebrow and waited for Wade to answer.

Wade couldn't have come up with an answer for that with all the time in the world. He was still thinking as Sean left through the gate, his chuckles trailing behind him. Wade slipped into the water to cool off and immediately snagged his daughter's hands to zoom her around the deep end. Thea stuck to the shallows as ordered by her mother, but she loved to go fast. Then he showed her a shallow dive off his bent knee and clapped when her head bobbed above the water like a cork.

"Thank you for getting a pool, Daddy," she yelled. Wade put one finger over his mouth to remind her to lower her voice but held the burst of happiness that washed over him tightly. "Oh, right, the neighbors," Thea said in a stage whisper.

"Yes, we want to be good neighbors," Wade said before he allowed her to push him under the water and blew explosive air bubbles up. She was giggling when he resurfaced.

They'd never made it to this point when he'd been picking her up for too-far-apart visits.

This was everything he'd missed. Before he could get too sappy, Thea had ducked her head underwater, the rest of her skimming the surface, as she kicked and splashed over to the side of the pool.

Wade decided to check his phone for texts. Since his ex and her new husband had flown out of Miami early that morning, he was going to need a babysitter for this date. He'd texted and Vanessa should be sending her babysitter's name and number.

"Daddy, time me. How long can I stand on my hands?" Thea yelled.

Wade obediently held up his phone. "Go."

He lost track of how many times Thea tried to beat her previous record. He hopped out of the pool and relaxed in the comfortable lounger he'd chosen for the judge's stand. While he very obviously did not turn to stare at Brisa and make a big deal out of her arrival, he considered whether or not he was surprised that she'd followed through on joining them.

Then Wade realized he'd expected to see her. No matter how many times she'd given him only part of the truth or none of it, Wade still believed her. Did that mean he was getting to know Brisa or was he too gullible to live in this world?

The first drip of water hit his leg and he yanked his phone out of the way. Thea stood before him, twisting her hair in one hand and waving at Brisa with the other.

Wade noticed that Brisa had spread out a shocking pink beach towel. It set off the black swimsuit she was wearing to amazing effect. He knew in his heart she'd planned that carefully, but it didn't eliminate any of the impact. If anyone needed a model for summer fun, Brisa was perfection.

He should have picked a different T-shirt. The one he was wearing advertised the local hardware store. He'd gotten it for free after his who-knows-how-many trips. It was gray. So were his trunks. He matched, but no one would want to take his picture.

"Dad." Thea had bent closer to him, dripping all the way. Her exasperation made him wonder how many times she'd already repeated herself. "Dad!"

"What did I miss?" he asked and put one hand on her shoulder to urge her to take one step back.

"Do you think she would want to play a game?" Thea tangled her fingers together and twisted back and forth. "In the pool?"

The shadow that fell across his legs alerted him that Brisa had moved closer.

"Actually, I was coming to ask if you wanted to have a race," Brisa said.

"Me?" Wade asked as he watched the pink plastic rings she was waving.

The long pause got his attention. Finally.

"No. Not you. I want someone who'll give me a challenge." Brisa pointed at Thea. "My sister and I used to have races across the pool with these. We need some-one to throw them for us. If your dad says okay, do you want to?"

Brisa waved the rings and they clacked together.

"We have to stay in the shallow end." Thea pointed. "I can only be in the deep end if my dad's in the water. Mom's rules.

Dad's gonna teach me to swim better but we only started today."

"Mom is a smart lady. There's plenty of room in the shallow end." Brisa handed Wade the rings. "You throw them when we say. Got it?"

If anyone forced him to tell the truth, he would admit that he was only following her lead. Brisa, sparkling down at him, in her swimsuit with the lush foliage around the pool as her backdrop had short-circuited all his synapses. Then his brain kicked in, and he fought back a groan as she blinked patiently at him. Women as smart and beautiful as her should come with a warning.

"Got it, boss." He took the rings. "Sorry, I'm slow on the uptake this afternoon."

Brisa smoothed her hair over one shoulder. "Happens to me a lot. I'm used to it." After she waggled her eyebrows at him, she took four steps backward and fell into the deep end. Gracefully. Somehow, Brisa made even that look lovely and artistic.

Thea let out a warrior yell and jumped into the shallow end.

Wade moved closer to the side and

watched them both surface. Brisa immediately dove under the water and the floating divider to move into the shallow end. "Okay. Let's do an easy one first. We'll both start at the wall. Dad will throw one ring and we'll race to get it." Brisa pointed at the wall where Wade stood.

Thea nodded wildly, and Wade could tell by the spark in her eyes that this was going to be the first of countless races. He grabbed his phone, fully expecting a timing element to be included, and sat down to dangle his feet in the water.

"We're ready when you are," Brisa called out from her spot near his right knee. Her hair was a sleek curtain. The perfection of her face, no shadow or lipstick or any of the usual tools, was impossible to ignore.

"When I say go…" Wade met her stare. The tears were gone, and she was happy in that moment.

Playing pool games with his daughter.

If that didn't change a man's mind about a woman, nothing would. Whether he'd already forgiven the catfishing or not, there was no way to hold on to the irritation now.

"Go!" He tossed one single ring. "First

one to get it wins." Instead of jumping into the churning race, Brisa squeezed his knee, giggled at the way he jumped and then gracefully lost the race.

CHAPTER THIRTEEN

BRISA GAVE WADE'S daughter a high five for winning their latest competition. As she caught her breath after doing a handstand in the shallow end of the pool, she shared a quiet laugh with Wade. Someday, Thea McNally was going to give Mira Peters a run for her money as the strictest personal trainer on the planet. Wade's daughter did not hesitate as she dreamed up new combinations of races and feats of strength.

It was also more fun than Brisa had experienced in a pool since her sister had gotten too old for their competitions. Lap swimming might be more adult, but she wasn't sure it was a better workout than meeting the challenge of Thea McNally.

The calculating gleam in Thea's eye was warning that she'd dreamed up a doozy.

"How much do you know about synchronized swimming?" Thea asked, a small frown communicating how seriously she took the question.

Before Brisa could frame an answer that captured both "absolutely nothing" and "willing to learn," Wade's phone rang. "Thea, let Brisa rest now. We need to get out and eat some dinner soon." Then he stood and answered his phone. "Hey, you could have texted. I didn't expect a call." He moved away, so it was harder to eavesdrop and Brisa knew Thea was watching her closely. At her father's words, Thea had sat down on the steps, her shoulders hunched. She would follow his directions, but it would take self-control and a theatrical long-suffering expression.

Thea reminded Brisa of herself. It was both cute and alarming. Wade was going to be facing an ongoing battle of wills.

"I don't know anything about synchronized swimming," Brisa said. "Do you?"

Thea brightened. "You can win medals and look so beautiful. You get to wear bright red lipstick. I'm going to do that before I go into space. It'll be harder to do it after, I think."

Brisa pursed her lips as she considered

the proper order to become a world-class athlete and astronaut. "You could be right."

"Let's practice our sculls. Want to? I can show you! This is a stationary scull. Watch. You need to know how to do it so you can stay afloat while you're upside down in the water." Thea immediately tossed her floaty to the side of the pool. Then her head was underwater while her legs were perfectly straight and her arms moved close to her sides. Thea didn't move, and Brisa realized that was the measure of a successful stationary scull.

There was also no way Brisa would be able to copy it.

"It's a long travel day, I know. You could have texted me the babysitter's phone number." Wade met Brisa's stare as he checked on Thea. "Thea's practicing her sculls, like she threatened to."

Brisa heard whoever was on the other end say, "Show me."

Wade fiddled with the phone and then turned it to face Thea's legs, capturing Brisa nearby. Even from the distance, Brisa was almost certain the woman was Wade's ex. The woman's eyebrows shot up and she said, "Wade McNally, turn me around right now."

Thea popped back up out of the water. "Good, right?" Brisa nodded and heard the caller say, "You did it! You did it! I'm so proud of you. You asked her out, didn't you?" The last part was high-pitched, a happy squeal.

Wade met Brisa's stare and cleared his throat. "Uh, no, she's Thea's new synchronized swim partner and she's listening." Whatever she would have said in response, he covered by adding, "But I do have a date on Saturday with someone else. That's why I was asking about a babysitter. A couple of hours in the morning, maybe lunch. That's all. If you'll text me the number of the neighbor you usually call, that's all I need. You can go back to honeymooning in whatever European airport you're currently in."

"Take me off speaker or face-thing or whatever right now. I need to talk to you," his ex-wife said.

Was he in trouble? That was the tone, but Brisa wasn't sure.

"My mom and Steve are going to Japan

for a honeymoon now that Daddy's here. It takes a long time to get there." Thea shrugged as if it made perfect sense. Brisa nodded again. That did make sense, and Wade had already mentioned his ex's suggestion that he start dating again.

The desire to know what else Thea's mom was saying while Wade listened patiently burned.

"My mother hates water deeper than the bathtub. Steve loves swimming but he'll never be a good swim partner. He can't stay still in the water," Thea said sadly.

"Mommy wants to talk to you, Thea." Wade held out his hand and pulled Thea out of the water. He picked up a towel. "Dry off for a minute and then find out how her trip has been."

"They've only seen airports. I didn't know they could be exciting," Thea said, but she followed directions and then settled down in his seat for a chat.

"I once ran through the airport in Atlanta with one shoe on because I had five minutes to make a connection and no time to waste stopping when a heel broke. Airports come with stories, most of them terrible."

Brisa hoisted herself up to sit beside Wade. "No more swimming today?"

"For a guy who spent a lot of time on boats and in water, I enjoy pool time a lot less than you'd think. Give me an ocean, and I'll get serious." Wade grinned. "While Thea dreams of gold medals for swimming and who knows what she'll set her sights on tomorrow."

"She is a dreamer and the plans she makes…" Brisa tried to imagine ever thinking that big and couldn't remember doing it. "I love it."

"You would. You're a lot alike, always thinking, planning, improving." He sighed. "I'm happy to have this time with her, but keeping up? I'm not sure I have it in me. If you hadn't been here, there would have been an argument and tears because I might have chased that ring once or twice, but you lost…so *many* times."

Hearing his assessment of her caught her off guard. He thought she was like Thea? When they first met, she'd been certain Wade was one more person in the world who would always be either faintly patronizing or prepared for her to fail.

Like her sister after she first came home.

Or worse, loudly state his disapproval of her decisions.

Like her father.

Wade kept showing her that wasn't who he was.

After a lifetime, Brisa had built up a thick skin to hide the disappointment and hurt, but inside, it was harder to ignore the little girl who was always on the wrong step. Even if the adults in Thea's life were doing a good job of encouraging her, not trying to make her dreams smaller.

If Wade McNally believed she was always working to improve things, then... Brisa bowed her head. It was too much to grasp in that moment. "Thea explained why I lose so often. I'm still in training. She'll have me whipped into shape soon."

They both laughed, and it was so simple, so sweet, to be lazing at the pool, talking with a handsome guy who lifted her spirits effortlessly. How nice it could be to have this contentment always.

Wade kicked his legs slowly in the water. "Could you text Mira my number and ask her to call me? I have to reschedule Saturday. Vanessa's babysitter is on vacation, of all things." He grunted. "She won't cut short her trip to Hawaii to help me out."

"A babysitter, something else it would be good to have a recommendation for if we're going to bring families to Concord Court. I need to make a note." Brisa pretended to scribble in her binder as she tried to come up with a name, someone who was good with kids and available, but the only person she could come up with was Mira, the other person on the date. "I should have considered the babysitting question when I was making your plans. Sorry about that."

Brisa wasn't in the habit of worrying about childcare since most of her friends were even more single and free than she was.

"I've decided it's a good thing, to take more time with this. I was in such a big hurry to get out there, to find someone, because I wanted to get my life together before I started the new job." Wade held his arms out to show how big the problem was. "What was I thinking? I loved being married to a great woman and it still managed to fall apart. Did I really believe all

I had to do was put my mind to it, all that logic would make it quick and easy?" He laughed. "I've lived most of my life without family, so it's become my only goal. Rushing will lead to another mistake and I can't have that. I'll have to be patient." He expelled a harsh breath. "Shut up, Wade. This is what it sounds like in my head, one question, three different things to analyze, which lead to six more questions, until I'm worn-out by thinking."

"May I suggest my patented binder system? Writing it down can get it out of the head," Brisa said with a grin. Then she bumped her shoulder against his. He was hard to read most of the time. Tonight, he was open in a new way. Foster care was beyond her knowledge, but she understood the need for family. She loved hers, even if she wondered where she fit sometimes.

And she knew about that hurry he'd been in to solve everything at once. For her first few weeks at Concord Court, she'd been convinced she'd have it all under control by the end of the next week…except the next week kept moving farther and farther out and she was still scrambling.

Getting hit with two grant rejections on the same day had knocked her feet out from under her.

But Wade's babysitting problem? That, she could fix. Brisa clapped her hands. She'd spent almost zero time in charge of children and might regret making the offer, but he needed help. She could help, so she should help. "If it makes you feel any better, I've also learned that naming your problems aloud can help with the answers." She batted her eyelashes at him. "I'm off this Saturday. Thea and I can kill a couple of hours if it will nudge true love along its way. I haven't been to the science museum since Pluto was still considered a planet."

Thea sat up straight. "The science museum? Could we go?"

Wade frowned as he studied Brisa's face. The longer it took him to respond, the more certain she was that he was evaluating her skills and they didn't measure up.

"I can't ask you to do that. It's too much. And the physical demands are intense. You lose a lot of races. What if Thea is kidnapped by a rogue dolphin? Who would save her? Not you." He shook his head slowly. At close range, Brisa could see the small upturn in his lips as he teased her.

"I'll postpone the date until Vanessa's back. That's the smart thing to do," Wade added.

"Wade, go on the date. You're stalling because of cold feet. Give Thea your phone, some money, and send them both to the science museum," his ex-wife yelled through the phone.

Brisa wondered which airport they were in. Would loud Americans in a German airport make international news?

Wade pinched the bridge of his nose. He had to know he'd been outmaneuvered by his daughter again. "You're going way beyond the bounds of what can be expected of a leasing manager. I don't know you very well. I've always been good at handling problems, being self-sufficient, but now…"

Brisa waited for him to fill in the blank, but Wade only nodded.

As if the situation was too much to put into words.

"Ugh, you're just so…frustrating." Brisa let out a groan. This had been her biggest issue with Reyna, Sean and even Jason

Ward. When Jason first moved in and had to be talked into taking the job he was perfect for because he couldn't accept the help. And Wade was going to get in that line. "Why do you think you have problems no one else does? Really? People all over this world are hunting for babysitters even as we speak. You know what they do? They ask family and friends and neighbors… which you just did. Those family, friends and neighbors pitch in if they can. It doesn't have to be this soul-searching occasion on why you can't handle every single problem on your own."

Brisa realized she'd raised her voice and slipped down to dunk her head under the water. Clearly, she had to cool off.

When she surfaced again, Wade was watching her. "Got that off your chest now? Been holding it in for a while, I'm guessing."

She shrugged. "I'm right, though."

He sighed. "Yeah, you are."

His agreement landed with a soft glow right in the center of her chest.

It felt good.

"Thea, turn the phone back around," his

238 THE DOCTOR AND THE MATCHMAKER

ex-wife said loudly. When she was facing Brisa again, she said, "Give me your phone number, your address and your last name, Brisa." The woman smiled, but there was something wicked about it. "If anything happens to either one of these people I love, I'll find you."

Brisa blinked but rattled off the required information and nodded as Thea returned to her phone call.

"She seems nice. A little cutthroat. I like her." Brisa had never been introduced to Vanessa—that was her name!—but it was good to make that brief connection.

"I accept your help, friend and neighbor." Wade narrowed his eyes at her. "But I'm about to hit you with some truth, too. I'll turn down the volume because I appreciate your offer and *because they're listening*." He whispered the last part and waited for a second. "Look at me. This is going to be hard for you to hear." His voice had lowered as he bent his head closer and Brisa had to fight back the shiver that desperately wanted to sweep through her.

Would Thea rescue her from this weird... Was it attraction? Brisa hesitated to name it. She would lose ten more races to avoid whatever this was going to be. Thea had stretched out to talk to her mother.

With no way out, Brisa rested her elbow on the warm concrete. "Be gentle."

"I'll try," Wade murmured. "Ready?" He raised an eyebrow, so Brisa nodded. "You're doing a good job here." The direct compliment immediately triggered the cringe that lived below Brisa's skin. People could call her beautiful. She'd flirt that away, but this? So unexpected.

Wade continued, with his eyes locked to hers. "Those notes you made about our dinner conversation and ordering tea for me, so I don't have to explain being sober? That care is going to help me and who knows how many others. Babysitting? Not many people would make my problem theirs."

"Even fewer would lie on a personals website," Brisa chimed in, her lips twisted, as the urge to remind him how messed up she was spilled over.

"You sure about that?" Wade asked. "That's not coming up again, not between us. That means from you, too. Let it go. We are neighbors now, the end."

Brisa sighed. "I'm not great at letting anything go."

Wade reached down to squeeze her shoulder. "I understand that, but I'm telling you that you have to. You can follow orders, can't you?"

His lips quirked as her eyebrows shot up.

"Orders," Brisa muttered as she reluctantly joked. "Of all my failures, following orders is at the head of the list. You'll have to ask my father when that started, but I'm sure it was before I climbed out of my crib the first time."

They smiled at each other, bound in that moment, until everything else fell away. A kiss would have been magic, but Thea's giggle broke the spell. Brisa jerked back.

"Thea, wrap it up. We need food." Wade started to stand, but Brisa put a hand on his knee. Both of them froze until she moved back.

"I wanted to say thank you, for distracting me this afternoon. I needed it." Brisa raised her chin. "I let go of my sense of impending failure for at least an hour."

Wade stood and took the towel and the phone Thea held out. "No problem. Maybe someday we'll pass neighbors and make it to friends."

"I think we're already there," Brisa added softly as she waved at Thea, who darted through the gate, her father a step behind.

Then she dunked her head under the water again.

Something about the way *friends* rolled off her tongue felt wrong.

If it was because she was hoping for more, whatever the next step, it should be labeled Big Trouble.

CHAPTER FOURTEEN

ON SATURDAY MORNING, the day of the big date, Wade realized how little time he normally spent choosing clothes or fixing his hair or even staring in the mirror and really seeing himself. He wore gym clothes to the gym and scrubs at work. That was normal. He wasn't sure what to do to better his usual routine, especially for a date that would take place on bicycles. Dressing fancy didn't fit and casual seemed… too casual for a special occasion.

His daughter was seated at the bar enjoying the breakfast she'd finally agreed to after they ran out of milk for cereal: toast, orange juice, no bacon. Eggs and milk were on his grocery shopping list in bold capital letters.

"Thea, what do you think of this?" he finally asked when the uncertainty pushed him too far. "Okay for a first meeting?"

"You mean a date?" she asked in a sing-song. "Mom told me to make sure you didn't embarrass any of us on this date when I talked to her yesterday on the phone." Thea dropped her toast and came around the counter to study him carefully. When she twirled her finger to tell him to turn around, he considered lecturing her on the proper way to speak to her elders.

Then Wade realized he let his daughter call him by his first name sometimes. So he turned slowly around. Khaki shorts, lavender polo, canvas boat shoes. It was his only choice. If she didn't give him a passing grade, what was he going to do anyway? "I'm not sure this is a good idea. I could cancel." He would cancel except he'd have to text Brisa to take care of it because he still didn't have Mira's phone number.

Thea didn't respond as she judged him.

Who was going to help him improve his dating wardrobe? If this date didn't work out, he'd have to do it all over again.

Wade closed his eyes as he realized that, even if it did work out, he was going to have to answer this question again at some point. Either way, there would be more dates.

He needed a female fashion adviser.

"When your mom gets back home, we're all going shopping," he muttered. Vanessa was encouraging this. She'd love to put him through the misery of a fitting room, too.

When he faced Thea again, she nodded. "Solid plan, but you're good to go. You can wear this on my first day of school, too. You won't embarrass me when you drop me off." Her work done, she scrambled back up onto the stool at the bar.

Wade took a bite of his toast as he evaluated that. In a young girl's life, not being embarrassed at the morning drop-off was a high priority. That was a good endorsement of his choices today.

"What else did Mom say? Is the trip going well?" Wade asked.

Thea nodded. "They're leaving Tokyo today to go and meet up with Steven's parents. She seemed nervous."

Meeting the parents had to be a big deal. He'd managed it with Vanessa's before he and Vanessa had married, but he'd never had to introduce anyone to his family. His last foster mother had been gone for a long time when he and his ex said I do.

Then he realized Vanessa and Thea would be his important introductions. If they didn't approve, almost any relationship would be doomed.

For some reason, that connection made him happy. Some of the nerves disappeared. Having input might prevent him from making a wrong decision.

"Mom also warned me to be on my best behavior for Brisa, just in case." Thea sipped her orange juice and pursed her lips.

"In case of what?" Wade asked, even though he knew he didn't want to know the answer.

"In case you want to be more than friends someday." Thea raised her eyebrows and could have been her mother's twin in that second. "I explained that Brisa and I are already friends because we've started training together, so you should be the one afraid to mess that up."

Wade sighed. This was when he regretted having no adult backup at his side. His daughter was smart enough to render him speechless often.

They were quiet as they munched. Thea brushed her messy hair out of her face. Should he offer to put it up for her? He'd meant to study some hair tutorials online but had conserved his energy by napping often instead. His ponytails had gotten better. Stronger. Thea complained less about going bald, anyway.

"Just try to have fun and forget about your mother's advice. Are you excited about the trip to the planetarium? I've been meaning to take you to this science museum for a while," he said as Thea moved to the sink and waited while she rinsed the crumbs off her plate and put it in the dishwasher. His daughter had learned her mother's ways. No dishes in the sink. Ever. It was cute on Thea. Wade and Vanessa had loud disagreements at the end over everything, including the necessity of unloading the dishwasher, how to load it properly and the reasons that neat freaks were impossible to live with.

The shouting had been about so much more but fighting over the dishes had been easier.

Thea shrugged. "Sure. I wish you were

going, too, but I imagine I'll have lots of time to teach Brisa about the universe."

Wade chewed his last bite of toast to cover the smile. The wonders of the universe covered in three hours or less. Brisa was going to be exhausted when this was all over.

"When you get home, we'll pack your backpack for the sleepover tonight. Okay, Thea?" Wade injected as much enthusiasm as he could into the words, even though he wasn't feeling them.

"I was trying to forget about that." Thea studied her hands which were flat on the granite countertop. Almost as if she was afraid to look at him. "I could stay here if you need me to."

The urge to give her the easy way out was powerful. Wade picked up his juice glass and swallowed all the liquid. "Don't you have fun with Isabel?"

The way she nervously met his stare and looked away squeezed his heart. "Not as much fun as I have with you and Brisa."

Before he could warn Thea to take it easy on Brisa, the doorbell rang.

Brisa had held her own at the swimming pool. She'd be fine here, too.

He and Thea would pick up the conversation about the sleepover in due course. Wade could find her an easy way out between now and then.

As he opened the door, Wade realized how much anticipation was bubbling. He wanted to see Brisa. Cocktail dress, moving chic, jeans and a T-shirt and the Concord Court uniform—they all fit her perfectly, as if anything she wore was tailored for her.

He wasn't ready for the sundress or the strappy sandals. Brisa might as well have stepped off the pages of a fashion magazine. She pushed her dark sunglasses up into her loose, dark hair. "Morning. Who wants to go find some constellations?" Her tone was bright, almost aggressively chipper, as if she was pumping herself up, too.

He did. He wanted to go wherever they were.

But he'd asked for this date. He'd demanded this blind date, to be clearer. He was going.

"Not me. I want to ride a bicycle." Wade

motioned her in. "Thea is preparing her lecture for you even as we speak." Her shoulder brushed his arm as she moved past him. That simple accident, the slip of her warm skin against his, sent a wave of awareness through him.

So, he was headed out for a date with one woman but immediately felt more alive because of Brisa. That could be a problem.

"No lecture preparation needed. It's all right here." Thea tapped her temple.

Wade pulled out his wallet. "Money. It's for admission. It's for lunch." He stared from Brisa to Thea and back. "For both of you. Anything left over? Get a souvenir." He held the money tightly when Thea tried to take it. "Got it, Thea?" Brisa would be a better choice to handle cash, but this was one of those times. If he didn't support Thea here, what would that tell her about trust?

Her grumbled sigh was cute, but he didn't smile. Brisa did, and it brightened up the room. He wished he was going along to the science museum now to learn the origins of space and time, even though he'd heard it before. Brisa's presence made it new.

Mind on the matter at hand, McNally.

"Do you want to carry the money?" he asked. "Brisa has a purse. She can keep it, then you could even leave your backpack here for later."

Thea stared solidly up at him. "I have a backpack because I want to carry things. I'm not a baby."

Wade let the money go. Thea was right. She wasn't a baby.

The consequences of losing it or blowing it all on souvenirs were so low that it was an excellent time to give her the freedom. No matter what, Brisa would keep her safe.

Had they known each other long enough to know that as firmly as he did?

Wade wasn't sure, but Vanessa had given in easily. If his ex-wife, who was the expert in their parenting co-op, believed this was okay, he'd go along. His urge was to keep Thea under his eye, one arm around her shoulders at all times, but Thea would never accept that easily. She wanted to do too much, explore everything everywhere. Vanessa had learned to let go of her grip a little; he'd follow her lead.

Then he realized how quickly his own

opinion had changed. He'd expected Brisa to be shallow and vain; instead, she was trustworthy enough to take care of the person he loved most in the world.

He didn't want them to leave without him.

"Have you got a key?" Brisa asked Thea. "If we get back before your dad, you can use the time to explain dark matter to me."

Thea frowned. "I don't know much about dark matter."

"Unless it's literally the space between the stars, which looks dark to me, that's still more than I know," Brisa said cheerfully.

They watched Thea process that. "I have a key. If we have the time, I'll start with the Big Bang. That's as close to dark matter as either of us will get and I have a cool book with *pictures*."

Brisa narrowed her eyes as if they were negotiating. "Cool. You ready?"

When Thea held out her hand, Wade could see a hairbrush. His daughter was going to take matters into her own hands. "Braids, please." Then she presented Brisa with her back.

Without hesitation, Brisa flexed her fingers and started to work.

Wade tried to watch carefully. It seemed easy enough. Hair went over and under. Why did he end up with knots? In less than five minutes, Thea's hair was in two nice, neat braids that would clearly last a couple of hours at the planetarium.

His daughter didn't complain about having her hair pulled once, either.

Brisa didn't understand what she'd done. When she was finished, she offered Wade the hairbrush. "We're off. Have a great time on your date. Do not worry about a single thing. Thea is in charge of our excursion and Mira will take charge of yours." She winked at him over Thea's head, and after his daughter had stepped outside, Brisa motioned up and down to indicate his outfit and gave him a thumbs-up.

As if she was a friend, a supportive, encouraging, "uninterested in any romantic entanglement" friend.

Why was that depressing?

Then they were gone, and he had to leave to make it on time to the gallery in Wynwood. As he parked, he had no memory of making the drive over but most of his nerves had settled. He'd been busy imagining what Brisa would think of Thea's lectures and the planetarium show to remember his turns and stoplights.

Brisa did that for him over and over. He got tangled up with questions in his brain, let some of them spill out around her, and she worked through the knots with simple solutions, easy words and a bright smile. She didn't get frustrated, either. Some people might avoid him because, lately, he always needed a favor.

More than once, she'd taken the weight off his shoulders.

That was a nice talent to have.

Who did that for her? Wade shook his head. Now was not the time for pondering questions like that. He slid out of the car, locked it and moved around to the shaded sidewalk in front of a long strip of funky shop fronts, all painted in different colors, some pastel, some bright. Here and there, the walls were accented with spray-painted art. Bold. Graphic. Each image made up of fine details that were hard to take in with a single glance. From Wade's spot on the sidewalk, he could see the tip of what looked like a three-story building with a vintage Welcome to Miami postcard painted on the side.

As Wade walked toward the gallery, he found a pretty, petite woman with long dark hair evaluating everyone who walked by. The way she toyed with the end of the ponytail draped over her shoulder suggested she might be dealing with some nerves, too. She had to be his date.

"Mira?" Wade asked the woman. "Are you Mira?"

"You must be Wade," she said as she held out her hand. "Brisa told me to wait for the good-looking guy in the lavender shirt."

Wade shook her hand as he realized two things. First, Brisa had called ahead to soothe Mira's nerves, as well. She had planned everything to make this a success. Mira had known exactly who to expect. And second, Brisa thought he was good-looking.

Why did that matter? It didn't.

But it really did.

"So, this is the place." Mira pointed at the line of bikes in the bike rack in front of the neon yellow wall. "Should we go inside to get this tour started?"

Wade held open the door and followed her inside. There, a tall lanky blonde with a line of rings in both ears and a septum piercing raised one thin arm. "My tour has arrived. I was beginning to wonder if you'd chickened out. It's always the heat that gets people." She ran a hand through her spiky hair.

"Are we the only people on this tour?" Mira asked as she surveyed the small space. One wall was covered with a mural that reminded Wade of the Day of the Dead masks he'd seen, but these faces were all done in black and white roses vining in and out of each other. The background was a rich, deep blue.

"Yep, I don't usually start until late afternoon, since the nightlife around here draws good crowds, but Brisa asked me to add a morning tour. Something about giving some friends a treat." The woman pointed at them. "I owe Brisa a lot. She's my unpaid model for every catalog and the tour promotional shots on my website, so it was easy to say yes. I'm Vi. This is my studio. You're free to take a wander around after the tour. Let's get you on a bike." She jingled keys and then herded them toward the door.

It was easy enough to follow directions. Vi locked the door to the gallery behind them. Apparently, she was closed while they were out on their tour.

After a bit of trial and error, Wade and Mira were both fitted with comfortable bikes.

"Brisa called in a couple of other favors to make this super special for you guys, so we have some visits to make, but otherwise, if you see a piece you're interested in, we'll stop and I'll tell you what I know. If we can track down the artist, we'll do that, too." Vi took the lead. "This time of day, the sidewalks are less crowded. This is going to be fun. Let's start with the Wynwood Walls."

Wade and Mira rode behind in single file until the sidewalk opened up.

"I don't remember the last time I rode a bicycle," Mira said when he joined her. "Good thing it's as easy as riding a bike."

Wade nodded to acknowledge her

humor. Some of his nerves settled. She was meant for bright sunshine, her smile dazzling. Mira's beauty was easy, natural, tan skin and gleaming eyes, and the joy on her face made it clear she loved being out and moving.

He was lucky Brisa had convinced her to say yes to this blind date.

The tour's first attraction was a walled area formed by large warehouses where one art piece bled into the next. Vi gave a short explanation about the artists who worked there and then wandered discreetly away to wait by the bikes so that he and Mira could stroll at their own pace. That was probably intended to facilitate conversation. Mira was absorbed in the art and Wade was stuck for a clever opening.

This date was beginning to be familiar; most of his other dates had started this painfully awkward way, too.

When they got back on the bikes, they rode for a bit, past smaller studios, and stopped in front of a vibrant mural painted on a three-story brick building. Vi said, "This is one of the newest pieces. Carter has been working on this for months, but it's nearly complete. Do you recognize the faces?"

Wade couldn't count how many people stared back, but realistic portraits in tones of black and gray had been formed into letters on a background that started orange in the center and bled seamlessly into bright red waves. Together, the contrast spelled Unite.

"These are community leaders here in Miami," Vi said. "Some of the artwork in Wynwood is bright and fun, but every artist has a mission. There are organizers working for safer neighborhoods, better schools, legal protections for minorities. Carter supports the activists working to make Miami safe for all of us. This is his voice. That's the purpose of art, to be the voice. And graffiti is art here." She went on to discuss the media used, always spray paint, sometimes acrylics with rollers, and the other tools. The precision required to paint a portrait on the side of a building was impressive.

"It must take a lifetime to learn this," Mira murmured.

Vi shrugged. "Or maybe he's born with

it. Carter is twenty. And he is this good."
She wrinkled her nose. "Also a nice guy,
so it's hard to hate him for having natural
talent." She motioned them forward.

Wade realized how easy it was to enjoy
himself. Vi knew what she was talking
about. Mira asked smart questions. He
could listen. He could talk when he had
something to say. Most of all he reminded
himself to go with the flow.

Vi smoothed over the awkward first date
atmosphere.

Brisa might be a dating genius.

At the end of the first hour, Vi stopped
behind a gallery. "Brisa has two surprises
here." She rapped on the back door. A short
young man answered, his shaved head glis-
tening in the bright sunlight.

"Eh, Vi! Good to see you!"

"Here are your students, Carter." Vi
pointed at him and Mira. "I'll be back in
thirty, okay?"

He and Mira nodded.

Carter pointed to a box. "Brisa suggested
a painting lesson. Are you down?"

Mira clapped her hands. "That woman.
I love her! Of course, I want to try." She

turned to Wade, her happiness was contagious. It was no wonder Mira had so many friends. "Come on, let's paint a heart. What colors should it be?" She squatted and opened the flaps.

"What are our choices?" Wade bent down beside her at the box. He'd hoped that would make the decision easier, but no. There was a can of almost every color.

Carter handed Mira a pair of gloves, a mask and a can of red spray paint. "How about a rainbow heart? That will give you space to experiment with lines and bleeding and technique. Now, whatever size you're imagining, double it. Triple it. Graffiti needs to be big."

"I do use my hands to work, but this will be completely different than surgery." Wade slapped on his gloves. He immediately wished he had the words back. There was only one thing worse than a pompous jerk and that was a stick-in-the-mud who liked to tell people about his important career.

Carter whistled loud. "A surgeon painting on my gallery wall, that's something." He nodded. "Well, Doctor, I teach classes here and have students from all walks of life. It's my building and you have my permission to do your worst. The number of coats of paint on this wall means no hurricane will ever bring it down. Now paint."

Mira shook the can and then painted a heart as big as her arms could reach. Wade wasn't sure how they'd ever fill it in, but Carter stepped up and coached her through completing the first round. Then it was his turn. "Try orange." Carter handed him the can and then stepped back.

Wade experimented with the spray and the distance from the wall as he tried to make a clean line next to Mira's. He lost control of the flow once or twice but when he stepped back, he'd made a thick, colorful orange line.

"Not bad for a first time." Carter smiled.

Wade grunted, sure that Carter was only being kind to humor him. The kid was right. He deserved the teasing. "I never had much time for art classes, although my foster mom encouraged them. I was always into science."

"Is that right?" Carter asked.

"Landed in a strict foster care home at fourteen. No chance to get into trouble there. If I had, my foster mom would have booted me, and I had plans that included staying put. After I survived high school, I joined the Navy. Any artistic talent or urges to wreak havoc were squashed by Miss Rose and Uncle Sam."

Carter ran a hand over his forehead. "I was in foster care for some time, too. More than one Miss Rose tried to keep me in line. Might have had a different experience than yours, but now I have art."

Wade studied him. "Yeah. I'm glad for you. I'm proud of what I did for myself, too. It's not all bad, with the right people in your life, is it?"

Their eyes met. It was impossible to sum up life in foster homes, but they didn't really have to. Foster care could mean a lot of different experiences. He'd been lucky. Miss Rose had been tough. Hard. More about rules than mothering. Good preparation for life in the military. She'd had high expectations for all the kids who came through, but they were safe there. Wade had never bucked her system.

Carter, whatever he'd been through, had come out stronger on the other side, too.

He was starting his own journey now. According to Vi, he was making it count, too.

The silence ended when Wade added, "I do have a preteen daughter who watched me paint her room and demanded crisp lines, so I channeled her voice."

They all laughed at that.

Mira wrinkled her nose. "Oh, no, she's tough. My baby sister is like that, forever giving me advice on how to improve my life. Three kids already and she's not even thirty. The aunties always mention how happy Kamini is when we have family phone calls, so that I can be convinced to get married and give motherhood a try even as the biological clock alarm is ringing loudly, but I can't figure out when Kamini sleeps. Since I like to sleep, that is a problem." She flashed him a grin over her shoulder as she stepped forward to try yellow. Each line grew tighter and smaller as they worked toward the center. "What's your daughter's name?"

"Thea," Wade answered. "She's too smart for me."

Mira grinned. "Yes, I have a total of five nephews. Can you even imagine? They surprise me all the time. At the last birthday party I attended for Jackson, who was turning five, I learned that kids need computers. Not a computer, but plural. I have no clue what he's doing. Another tech genius in the making there."

"Are they all here in Miami?" Wade asked, grateful for easy conversation.

"No, one sister is in Raleigh. My father was Air Force, too, but when he retired, he and my mother made Miami home. She grew up here. One by one, my sisters have moved closer. I expect Saashi will also end up here." Mira closed her eyes. "My parents chose a house with an entire acre of land. We will need every bit of it when all the nephews converge for holidays. For us, there's one of those almost every week. Every country we visited or lived in had a holiday my father adopted."

"That is a lot of celebrating," Wade said as he tried to picture what a family gathering that size would look like, would *sound* like. Sprawling. Noisy. Like no holiday he'd ever celebrated, for sure. "Sounds amazing."

Mira snorted. "Until you all have to use the single bathroom. Then it's dangerous."

They traded colors off until they completed the center. When he and Mira stepped back, Vi had returned. "Love it. Great students, huh, Carter?"

Carter nodded. "Brisa said they would be. Both are military, used to following orders. Both are smart and like a challenge." He took back the last can of paint Mira handed him. "Gotta trust Brisa. She knows people."

Wade shook Carter's hand. "Thanks for the lesson." Wade realized Carter's words hit the nail on the head. Brisa was able to accomplish all she had, including setting up this perfect date for the guy she'd tricked and convincing him to trust his most important person to her for safekeeping, all because she knew people. She understood them because she took the time. Now he owed her so much, but if he was reading Brisa correctly, she'd never see it that way.

"Painting was more fun than you expected, right?" Carter asked, one corner of his mouth curled up.

Wade propped his hands on his hips. "For someone with no artistic talent? Yes."

Carter rolled his eyes. "Because you

don't look for it and build it up doesn't mean you don't have the skill, my man." He shooed them back toward their bicycles. "Finish your date. Fall in love or don't. I've heard that's a talent, too, but what do I know about *that*? I like my freedom."

Wade enjoyed Mira's laughter as they pedaled out of the busy lot. "I wonder if Carter knows what he's talking about. Is falling in love a talent?" Mira asked as she kept looking ahead.

"I have no good advice there, so we'll have to trust Carter," Wade answered. "He's still young enough to know everything."

Mira nodded. "Yes, we used to be certain about everything, too."

Vi motioned them toward a small courtyard. It was the outdoor seating area to one of the restaurants they'd passed earlier. Tall trees provided enough shade that it was probably popular with the late afternoon crowd. Asphalt changed over to bricks, giving the place an old-world atmosphere. Large terra-cotta pots filled with orange and yellow flowers lined the alley's edge. Had Brisa set up lunch for them, too? She was better than a fairy godmother.

"This place serves the best sangria in the world, not that I've tasted all the sangria, but it's really good here." Vi pointed at a shaded table. "Brisa asked them to set up a quiet spot in case you wanted to talk. If you do, I'll leave you here. Turn left at the end of the alley and then right at the next street to return to my gallery. If you don't want to chat…" Vi paused as if she couldn't figure out what came next.

"Thanks, Vi, we'll catch up with you," Wade said as he put the bike's kickstand down. "We can't pass up the best sangria in the world." Well, he would, but it was still a nice gesture.

Vi waved and rode away.

"Mira, I hope it was okay that I made the decision." He hadn't hesitated, either. "Brisa thinks of everything."

Mira shook her head as she took a seat at the little bistro table in the shade. Two icy pitchers were sweating in the center of the table, and a waiter brought out a small tray of sandwiches and fruit. "She does think of everything. I was worried when she and Reyna explained how they were going to change managers at Concord Court. Reyna's tough and strong, the kind of leader that you understand why you're following. It's natural. And the Court ran smoothly, even through construction, but it's hard to argue with the ideas Brisa's coming up with." Mira picked up the dark red pitcher. "This business lab is going to take some time, but I've listened to Marcus Bryant talk about all his trouble getting his business off the ground, so I know it can make a lasting difference." She motioned to his glass.

"I'm going to have the other pitcher." It was water. It was icy. It would hit the spot. "I'm sober. No sangria for me."

Mira pursed her lips before pouring her own glass and setting the pitcher down.

"Sober, huh?" she asked before taking a sip and then sighing happily. "Want to get into that?"

Wade twisted his glass on the table as he considered that. If this was leading somewhere, he should. He met her stare, studied her friendly, interested face and felt no desire to explain. "Not really. I don't drink. Haven't for almost two years, and I'm better for it."

Mira's expression was serious as she accepted that. "Fair enough."

While Wade considered generic topics for discussion, like favorite books, movies, colors and sports teams, Mira chose a sandwich, took a bite and then said, "What I don't get is why you have Brisa setting you up. You can't have known her for long, so it's not like you're old friends who know each other so well." She took another bite, her eyes serious as she studied him. "Brisa went to a lot of trouble. This was no simple introduction. She joined my running group at dawn to make a good impression, then she agreed to keep running with me in exchange for getting me here." She plopped the last of the sandwich in her mouth and leaned back, as if she was prepared to wait however long it took for him to confess all his secrets.

Mira was comfortable here. At some point, her nerves had gone. His had, too.

Under other circumstances, that might be a good sign. Wade was almost sure it meant neither one of them was too worried about this working out well enough for a second date.

He couldn't confess all his secrets, because he'd promised Brisa, so he went for a piece of the truth. "Now that I'm settled here in Miami, I want to give marriage another try." That was the absolute truth. "I liked having a family. My first wife couldn't be happy with Navy life. I get that." He cleared his throat. "I also have all this history, the places I've served, a demanding job with bad hours. It would be nice to find someone who understands those demands and isn't intimidated by the challenge. I don't want to fail again. When I explained that to Brisa, she decided to introduce me to you." He skipped some details in the middle, sure, but it was basically true.

Mira stared out across the small patio as she considered that. "History. It covers so much ground." She straightened her shoulders. "I assume somewhere in there is the foster family and the sobriety that you don't want to dig any deeper into today."

"Yes, the terror of surgery under terrible conditions, the life-or-death decisions required that don't always go the right way, and the panic that hits without warning and sometimes feels as if it will never end. There are a lot of reasons why finding the right woman is a challenge." Wade squeezed his sandwich to pieces. "That's a lot to cover on the first date."

"And that's why you wanted to meet someone with a military background. Right?" Mira raised an eyebrow. "Brisa explained how I was the perfect choice. Air Force medic for a Navy surgeon, science teacher for a doctor. If anyone can understand that history, it's me."

Wade agreed. "You also like kids. Thea is a science geek who plans to revolutionize space someday."

"On paper, we are perfect." Mira shook her head as she swirled her glass. "If only I was looking for a relationship of any kind or you were really looking for me."

Wade was confused. "Oh. Why did you agree to the date, then, if you aren't looking, either?"

"Nope. Not looking," Mira muttered. "I didn't tell Brisa that, so she's innocent. I'm not available, not that anyone at Concord Court knows that. I have a husband. I don't talk about him." She wrinkled her nose. "I might have some history of my own."

Wade absorbed that. A secret husband. He had to laugh. Mira's grin was sheepish. "I hope you aren't disappointed. Brisa is so hard to say no to. And this was an amazing day."

After three of the tiny sandwiches, Wade laughed again. "I'm not disappointed at all. It was a fun morning and I needed one date with the training wheels on. I know a woman at the hospital was hitting on me, and the idea of it, on top of everything else, was almost too much for me to handle." He waited for her to acknowledge his pun. "It'll be easier the next time. Dating shouldn't lead to panic attacks."

At least he would know what to wear.

"Panic? How did you manage to get married the first time if random women give you anxiety?" Mira asked, her eyebrows sky-high.

Wade decided it was a fair question. "Alcohol helps, Mira. It gives many men false confidence. Without it, I'm…" He held his hands out. He was on a blind date he'd extorted someone else to set up with a woman who was already married. This one date was an excellent representation of his dating skills.

Her grimace was sympathetic. "That should make it so much easier to find the right one. Maybe. You meet her, you talk to her, and she'll be the one who'll get you, just you, no drinking."

Wade shrugged. It was a nice thought. Lots of women were easy to be with. That didn't mean he wanted to kiss them.

As soon as they stood, the waiter who'd been hovering in the shade came forward to clear the table. Wade and Mira walked their bikes back to Vi's gallery.

Mira said, "I don't know much about your history. I only know about insomnia, and the fact that almost every condition we might have due to our *history*—" she hit the word hard "—can cause it. There's an informal group that meets at the pool around midnight on those long nights if you ever need to talk or listen or not be alone. All veterans. All with history. Some of them will annoy you and there is always beer, but every person there will have your back."

Wade listened, but he wasn't sure what his response should be. He'd done fine handling his own issues, hadn't he?

"Yes, you've been able to handle things alone but that doesn't mean you have to." Mira paused. "No, you didn't say it aloud. I've got this particular script memorized."

Wade felt relief. "This is why I'd like to be with a woman who shares our background. It's so much easier to talk when someone else helps fill in the blanks."

Mira pursed her lips. "I was going to let it go, but earlier you said 'either,' in an 'I'm not available, either' way. Now I'm curious who the first choice was." She tapped her chin as she considered the problem.

"It was always this hazy goal, that's all. No one in particular," Wade said easily and hoped it worked, because Mira was every bit as sharp as Reyna had been and if she pondered too long, she would come up with the right answer. It no longer bothered him, but he didn't want Brisa to be embarrassed or have any trouble with her sister over something so small as the personal ad she'd posted with the best intentions.

Mira kept walking. "Honestly, I thought

finding someone who'd lived on an Air Force base would make life easier, too, but…" She crossed her arms over her chest. "That's no guarantee you'll be on the same page, Wade. It would be much better for you to find the woman who wants to know that history, who can listen and understand, one that you trust to carry it with you. Being with someone who has the same baggage is no use if they aren't able to help carry it all."

Then she rolled her eyes. "Deep thoughts for a fun Saturday."

Since it was clear her words were tied to something very deep and very much personal, Wade laughed. That was what she expected. They'd landed back in front of the bike racks. Wade waved through the window at Vi so that she could come lock them up.

Mira wrapped her arms around his neck for a hug. "Come join us at the pool. Friends can help carry all that stuff, too. I wouldn't trust a single one of those guys to set me up, so take any introductions they give you with a grain of salt. Sean Wakefield won over Reyna so he might have a bit of sense, but I wouldn't trust it too far."

Wade grimaced. "He's the one who suggested you to Brisa for this date."

Mira's mouth dropped open, then she snapped it shut. "Guess I should have told them about my little husband problem but…" She sighed. "They're going to give me such grief when I do tell them." She covered her face with both hands. "You know how it is with secrets. Some of them grow sillier the longer you keep them."

Wade squeezed her shoulders. "Grief, yes, but Sean thinks the world of you. They're your friends." He nodded when she turned to him. "It's your news to tell, not mine. As far as I'm concerned, we learned we'd make good friends. The end."

He had another secret to carry, but it didn't bother him a bit.

He walked her to her car and waited. "Brisa started running to get you to agree to this?" he asked.

Mira nodded. "Yep. It surprised us all. Her, too. You must be pretty important to her."

Or smoothing over the wrinkle between them was.

Mira started to get into her car but stopped. "I don't want to tell you your business, Wade, but if you want a woman who understands people, who can listen and be there for you, and who we know is good with kids, especially after today... You might consider Brisa." She raised her eyebrows at him but slid into her car before he could answer.

What would he even say?

Brisa was not in his world. She was in Reggie Beaumont's world, the Montero world.

Even if everything Mira had said about her was true. What would it take to convince himself that he was the man for Brisa Montero?

CHAPTER FIFTEEN

"I LOVE THIS PLACE. So much." Thea McNally waved her arms in the air of the spacious café nestled in the back of the science museum. Sunlight poured in from overhead skylights and the long line of windows showed an unbroken mat of green grass. "I could live here."

Brisa enjoyed the innocent and uncontained joy on Wade's daughter's face. Thea hadn't learned to worry about what other people thought of it yet. "You required a pool when you moved into Concord Court. I guess the aquarium counts here?" She checked her phone for the time. "Why don't you have every exhibit memorized? I know this isn't your first visit." Her plan had been for one planetarium show. Thea had changed that to two shows.

Only hunger pains had stopped her from pressing for more.

Brisa's phone showed no texts, no messages. Concord Court was fine without her.

So was Wade's date, apparently. Brisa put her phone facedown. He and Mira were having a good time. Why didn't that make her happier?

What would she have done if either one of them had backed out at the last minute?

Since she'd had to force herself to walk away from Wade that morning, Brisa might have celebrated. Then all three of them would be here. Together.

"Last year, I came with my class." Thea shrugged before she took a bite of her salad. "We had to stay together, and the class voted to explore the fish in the aquarium. Fish are smart. Water is for swimming in, not pointing and banging on glass to get the shark's attention." Her tone made it clear how silly she knew that was. Stars would always win in her book.

"I agree. Banging on glass is always a bad idea." Brisa reached for her phone again but forced her hands into her lap. "Who's your best friend at school?" Before picking Thea up, Brisa had wondered what they would chat about. Luckily, she and Thea were good talkers.

The way Thea's eyes darted to her face made her wonder if she'd touched a sore subject. As she recalled, girls Thea's age could fight over anything, but they were friends again the next day.

"Isabel, I guess, but…" Thea fiddled with her fork. "I'm not sure she likes me that much."

Brisa sat up straight in her chair. Someone didn't like Thea McNally? Unbelievable. Then she realized she was ready to go fight Isabel's mother over her daughter's poor judgment, and forced herself to relax. This kid was awesome. Everyone should see that. "Why would you say that?" There. Reasonable. She'd channel Reyna and pursue this line of questioning in an adult manner.

"She didn't invite me to her sleepover until my mother called her mother." Thea shrugged. "Sometimes I talk too much about things kids don't care about."

Brisa crumpled up her napkin and realized that Thea's confidence was less sturdy than she'd thought. "I get that. I have that trouble with some of my friends, too." She did. If she was throwing Daddy's money around, she had plenty of people to call. Buckling down to do a job had cut way back on those friends. Even Reggie would fade away soon. "What does Isabel like?"

Thea frowned as she considered that question. "Fish?"

Brisa bit back her smile. Thea was guessing. Had she ever taken the time to ask Isabel a question, or had she launched in the final frontier and talked nonstop?

"That's good. You know something about fish. You could talk to her about that." Brisa quickly continued. "If she likes fish, I bet she likes swimming." Was it true? Brisa was way out on a limb here, but she was going to follow it. "Do you think she has synchronized swimming talent?"

Thea blinked. "We've never had a pool to practice, but now I do. She could visit me when I'm at Daddy's and we could give it a try." She chewed her salad as she worked it through in her head. "I'll ask her tonight at the sleepover. Good idea, Brisa."

Brisa winked and sipped her tea, forcing herself not to stare at her phone.

"Did you know they had a show about dark matter when you said that this morning or do you know something about space?" Thea's eyes were locked on Brisa's face. The answer was important.

In the past, Brisa might have tried to impress Wade's daughter by rattling off the few bits she'd managed to pick up. Why it mattered so much that Thea McNally thought well of her when Brisa could barely remember meeting another child her age before deserved some reflection. Later.

Along with why successfully setting Wade up with someone as great as Mira didn't feel like a win. It was too easy imagining them falling into a friendly, easy love and it burned at the same time.

"I researched the museum before I picked you up this morning. I wanted to impress you. Dark matter sounded spacey, so I guessed you'd be interested." Brisa waved at the open café. "I like it here, too. Can you imagine how bored you would be stuck in my place or yours for hours on end?"

Thea frowned. "We could be at the pool. I like the pool."

"Your nose is already peeling from so much time in the sunshine. It's good to have other hobbies." Brisa took the last bite of her garden salad, chosen more to impress Thea than to answer any hunger pains. She'd almost ordered the chicken salad sandwich. Her vegetarian friend would not have approved. "When you're my age, you might thank me for saving your skin a little sun."

"When I'm your age, skin cancer will be cured." Thea's matter-of-fact tone was cute. Brisa hoped her optimism was rewarded.

"What about fine lines? Aging? Don't you watch enough television to know that women of a certain age, like me, and you someday in the very distant future, should avoid the appearance of getting older?" Brisa asked, curious about her reaction. Thea McNally had no intention of pretending to be interested in things that didn't matter to her. What would she say?

Her response: a long look of rebuke.

"Good answer, Thea. I like it." Brisa held up her hand for a high five. When

Thea laughed, Brisa added, "Spend plenty of time in the sunshine, but learn to love other things, too. I used to come to the museum when I was in school. Back in the ancient days, the space was smaller, and the technology—not so much, but that's all changed. I was always fascinated by archaeology, how the past is literally under our feet if we can find it." Brisa sipped her drink. "I felt like I was flying through space today."

Thea nodded wildly. "Yeah. It's too bad you're too old to be an astronaut. It would be fun to go to space with a friend."

Too old to be an astronaut. Brisa had to bite her lips as she shoved the rest of her salad away. That would put a woman in her spot, for sure.

Then she realized Thea had said "friend." They were friends.

How fun it would be to have a front-row seat to Thea's adventures. "You know who's not too old? Isabel." Brisa waved her fork at Thea to encourage her to make another effort with the fish fan.

Brisa watched Thea finish her salad, amazed all over again at how mature

Wade's daughter was most of the time and how easy it was to be with her. Thea didn't pretend or cover up her emotions; she lived loudly and with her heart on her sleeve. Here, she was swinging her legs in her chair in a manner that would have irritated Brisa's father, the rhythmic thump of her heels hitting the legs loud enough to hear.

How did Brisa know it would annoy Luis Montero? She'd initiated more than one experiment to prove it. Growing up, Brisa had learned early how to push his buttons. He didn't listen, so she made sure to get his attention any way she could.

Maybe he hadn't been the only one who could have made their relationship easier.

"How do you know you want to be an astronaut?" Brisa asked. Could this kid explain how to pick a career? Brisa had fought to win her spot at Concord Court but teetering on the edge of failure made it tempting to admit defeat and walk away.

That wasn't going to happen this time. She might have landed on her last chance to redeem herself in her family's eyes.

Thea frowned. "I don't remember where I got the idea." She shrugged. "I don't understand why everyone doesn't want to go to space. It's beautiful. I can imagine my life there and not here."

Brisa gathered up their trash as she evaluated that. At nine, Brisa had imagined modeling, acting, seeing new cities and doing exactly what she wanted when she wanted to do it. She'd done it all, too. Now every part of her imaginary future took place at Concord Court.

Parts of her plan for the next stage of her life were hazy, but she could easily make out the backdrop. Wrought-iron fence around a sparkling pool. A spacious office with a heavy oak desk. Sean and Reyna grossing her out with cuteness; her father and Marisol were hazy on the periphery.

Reggie didn't make the picture.

"Should we go check on your father?" Brisa asked. Unless she presented a good alternative, Thea would push for sitting through the next show at the planetarium, too. And Brisa was planning on keeping both feet on the ground.

Thea nodded. "After we stop at the gift shop. I have money to spend." She tapped her backpack and led the way.

Brisa didn't laugh out loud, but it was nice to find something they truly had in common.

They browsed in the shop for the perfect souvenir for some time. Thea eventually picked a glow-in-the-dark water bottle because it would be "easier to find in the middle of the night" and a book about string theory that Brisa asked zero questions about. She had no clue how anyone other than rocket scientists would read or understand it, but Thea opened it as soon as they got in the car and started flipping pages.

There were pictures. Maybe Brisa should borrow it sometime.

Watching Thea read while she drove tickled her memory of once doing the same.

They'd almost made it back to Concord Court when Thea asked in a distracted tone, "Why don't you want to go out on a date with my dad?" She didn't look up from the book in her lap, so Brisa had a minute to close her mouth and gather herself.

The direct approach was Thea's MO. Brisa would have to adjust.

"Your dad is great but…" Brisa managed to stop at a light that had turned yellow. "Mira has a lot in common with him. I don't." She fiddled with her seat belt, which had decided to strangle her at some point on the drive. "I'm already dating someone."

Thea's head popped up at that. "Oh." She pursed her lips. "Is it serious?"

Brisa blinked and then took her foot off the brake when someone behind her beeped their horn. "No, it isn't. And that's why I like it." Was that even true anymore? It was what she'd told herself and her father more than once, but it wasn't satisfying this time.

"My dad is serious, but not always. Mom says he deserves to be as happy as she is with Steven. She was trying to convince me that his dating was a good thing, but I already knew that." Thea closed her book and slipped it into the backpack she'd faithfully kept up with all day long. "He missed a lot while he was in the Navy. He should have everything now. I like you." She propped her elbow on the window. "Wonder if there's enough shade over the pool to swim yet."

That glow that came from her approval washed over Brisa again. Thea was a tough customer. Her acceptance was sweet.

"You don't have to worry about your dad spending time with anyone you don't like. You're his favorite everything," Brisa said, even though she was tempted to let the conversation fade away. "You know that, right?" Wade's affection for Thea was obvious. He left no doubts how he felt, even if he was confused, alarmed or outright flabbergasted by his daughter.

"His favorite everything?" Thea frowned. "I don't know about that. We argue. He's too bossy, treats me like a baby, like this morning, saying *you* should carry *our* money. I have my own savings account." The kid ducked her chin in a "can you even?" expression. "He loves me anyway. Sometimes we had to go a long time with just phone calls, but he always told me how much he missed me." She shrugged. "He always remembered the things that mattered. Always. My birthdays, first day of school, the time I won second place for selling the most candy bars in the first grade." She wrinkled her nose. "My mom did all the work, so I didn't mind not winning the pizza party so much. My dad paid for my mom to order pizza anyway. He was still in South Korea. I never visited him there because it's so far and I was too little then."

Wade had made Thea a priority, even when he was a continent away.

Thea argued with her parents, but she never doubted their love.

He was worried about his relationship with his growing daughter, probably because he felt guilty for not being physically near, but he'd always done his best. Thea knew that.

Brisa wondered if she'd ever considered that her own father had been doing the same thing.

"I mean, you should have heard Daddy cursing when he thought I couldn't hear while he was installing the system to control the lights in my new room. My mom?

She would have thrown everything in the box and sent it back. She would have been sorry, but she wouldn't have spent twenty minutes on hold to get tech support." Thea sighed. "I love her, but she is not good with tools or instructions. Now that they're both here, I can have it all."

Kids were so funny. She'd had no idea. Brisa couldn't help but chuckle at Thea's smug satisfaction. Wade and his ex-wife were raising a young woman who knew her worth, what she deserved and what she could accomplish. Divorce could have derailed that. Military life could have interfered. Their own flaws could have changed Thea's view of herself.

Brisa was learning how easy it would be to fall in love with a man who was this kind of parent. The ache in her chest was back, the gooey emotional melt that never happened when Reggie was around.

It was tempting to tell herself she deserved a man who made her melt.

What did Wade deserve?

More than a mess who depended on Daddy to live, for sure. Mira had proven herself through public service, and she was going to voluntarily surround herself with teenagers. Brisa would never measure up.

"Your dad and Mira had a great time together, I know it." Brisa could see Concord Court now, determined to enlist whomever she could to keep her friends plan for Wade and herself on track. "Let's help him figure out what to do on their next date, okay? We don't want him to lose any momentum."

As Brisa pulled into the parking spot in front of her town house, Thea unbuckled her seat belt and shook her head slowly. "Okay, if that's what you want. Whoever she is, she can't be prettier than you are. Best babysitter I've ever had. You've got natural swimming talent, too. I still think you're making a mistake. Guys like my dad don't come along often."

Reggie Beaumont was a professional athlete, successful in business and determined to give back to his community. Brisa could easily argue he was just as rare.

But men who'd treated her as a convenience instead of a priority? Too common.

Guys who valued her connections over

her brains, personality or even her looks, which had always opened doors? As hard to count as grains of sand in South Beach.

Frustrated with herself because she'd already settled this question, and the temptation to bump Mira out of the picture was a selfish urge old Brisa would have grabbed, Brisa slammed the car door too hard.

As she followed Thea down the sidewalk, she could see that Wade's car was already in the parking lot. He'd made it home before they had. Was that a good sign? The way the door swung open before Thea could knock meant Wade had been watching for them, waiting.

Brisa asked in her most friend-like tone, "Were you afraid I'd lost her? We had to stay for a second show, and then I was too hungry to go on without food." Plus, finding the right souvenir had meant a thorough search, but Brisa had no intention of ratting out Thea.

Or having to explain that the bag she herself was carrying included a Mars T-shirt and three pens that changed color and could write in space if she ever made it there.

Brisa had bought the loot after Thea told her she was too old to go to space because she refused to surrender so easily. Science would cure skin cancer and wrinkles some-day. Getting old astronauts into space had to be easier than that.

"No, ma'am, I knew she was in good hands. I missed her." Wade held his arms open and Thea launched herself at his chest.

The hard twist of jealousy in her gut sur-prised Brisa.

Their greeting was sweet.

She'd never had that kind of hello with any man.

"There was a show on dark matter, Dad. Brisa and I both learned a lot." Thea tossed her braids over her shoulders. "And the salad was pretty good, too, but look what I got!" She knelt on the floor and pulled out her book. "String theory. I'm going to learn so much."

Wade met Brisa's stare as he nodded. "Uh-huh, okay, good. I'll learn so much, too, I'm sure."

Thea blinked slowly. "You're welcome."

Wade looked skeptical. "Tell Brisa 'thank you.'"

Brisa was prepared to smile, wave and slowly fade away. Standing there and watching them caused that weird ache in the center of her chest to return.

Thea stood and wrapped her arms around Brisa's waist before squeezing. "You didn't have to take me to see the stars. I appreciate it."

Brisa had to clear her throat before she could answer. "I enjoyed every minute, Thea."

When Thea stepped back, she tilted her head to the side. "Think about what I said. About my dad." She waggled her eyebrows before picking up her bag. "I'm going to pack my stuff for tonight, Dad. Daylight's wasting."

She'd disappeared into her room before Wade could turn back to Brisa. "Are you exhausted? I'm sure she'd be happy to arrange more sculling practice if you'd like."

If she didn't get away from the McNallys soon, Brisa was going to make a fool of herself. Apart, they were great; together, they were devastating to her emotions.

"Thea's got that sleepover tonight, so there's no swim practice today. I did have an awesome time. I'm happy to babysit for your next date, too." Brisa leaned forward. "There will be a next date, right? I know I nailed it with this match." Why had she done so well the first time out of the gate? If she'd aimed lower...

Wade propped his hand on the door frame above her head. He wasn't blocking her escape, but his nearness robbed her of breath.

"Mira and I decided we make good friends. She invited me to join the group therapy session around the pool, if I ever decide to stop trying to handle all my problems on my own. Her words, of course." Wade's warm eyes studied her closely. "Still single, I guess. Want to give finding me a date another shot?"

Brisa licked her lips and wished for strength. "Disappointing. I knew you two would have so much in common, although she's absolutely right about that problem thing. Let the people who love you help. I understand that sometimes it can be too much, to need the help. I'm the unlucky one who always needs the help, but when I love someone, the sky is the limit for me. Whatever they need, I want them to have it."

Wade's lips curled, but he didn't step back. "Yeah, Mira and I talked about that, about how you understand people, how you make people's lives better."

Brisa jerked. "You talked about me? On your date?" That made no sense. She'd planned it carefully, so they had plenty of time and subject matter. Wynwood was one of the coolest neighborhoods in Miami and Vi knew the history.

"Shocks you to know people say nice things about you?" Wade asked.

"A little." Brisa straightened, her shoulder brushing against Wade's hand. "But I'm glad."

Off-balance, Brisa stared into Wade's eyes longer than she should have, but she couldn't step away.

What was happening between them?

"Mira is everything you promised. Smart and fun. It was a great day," Wade said with a sigh. "Neither one of us could have planned it better. Thank you."

Brisa tried a breezy wave, but didn't

quite manage it. "Don't mention it. It was nothing."

"That's just it. It's definitely something, Brisa." Wade raised his eyebrows. "Is that the kind of excellent planning Beaumont manages? Because if so, he's setting the standards very high, and the least he can do is write a how-to for the rest of us."

Brisa snorted and had to ignore the heat in her cheeks as his hair waved in the breeze she created. "No, Reggie might do dinner and a club or just the club. The end. He knows how to get the attention he wants there. Anything else? It's because I drag him along. If he has his cell phone and sports fans who want to talk football, he's happy. Extremely low-maintenance."

Wade studied her face. "You deserve more."

That was the realization that was slowly sinking in. She did deserve something more, something real.

Hearing it from Wade's mouth snapped everything back into focus.

"Reggie and I understand each other." Brisa looked away. "I know his limits. He handles my father. Our time together is easy, no stress, no big romance." That had been exactly what she wanted, too. Why didn't it seem enough right now?

"If that's true, he's a fool. A smart guy would be seizing his chance to make himself unforgettable."

Unforgettable? To her? She'd dated every kind of man. Actor. Model. Athlete. Rich kid. Entrepreneur. At least two lawyers and an accountant. All of them were forgettable.

"Honestly, now I'm the one who's lost. What is 'unforgettable,' Wade?" Brisa desperately wanted to know. If she took the risk and completed the total about-face of her life by ending things with Reggie and had to jump back in the dating pool, how would she recognize the "more" she deserved.

He was shaking his head as he moved closer. "I don't have words." His lips were a breath away from hers when he stopped. "But I hope this is the answer."

The alarms that should have stopped her never rang.

All the reasons she and Wade were wrong for each other slipped through her fingers as she squeezed his shoulders and pressed her lips to his. As their lips met, Wade's arms settled around her waist to pull her closer. Their lips joined easily, naturally, as if this was the sweet next kiss, not the awkward first kiss. He didn't let go but eased away from her. Their eyes locked, and neither spoke.

"I want to do that again," he whispered before sliding his lips across hers in a hot, quick follow-up.

Brisa wasn't sure when they would have moved apart without Thea interjecting.

"Can I take my mermaid sleeping bag tonight, Dad?" Thea yelled. Her shout from the bedroom convinced Wade to step back.

"Just a minute, Thea," he answered.

Brisa inhaled quickly. "Good thing she didn't catch us."

"Catch?" Wade asked as he propped a shoulder next to hers. "Like we're sneaking around or…"

Brisa rubbed her forehead, confused and uncertain and ready to slip back into his arms whenever they were open. "Um, on the way home, she suggested I was silly for not grabbing you for myself, no matter how good Mira would be."

Wade wrinkled his nose. "She's my biggest fan."

"She is. Whatever you're worried about with her, you're doing this right, Wade," Brisa said. "I told her about Reggie, so to find me kissing another man minutes later..." When she still wasn't actually single, even...

Oh, no. Reggie had even suggested a fake engagement to gain good PR to prod his team's management to sign his final contract. Reggie was a friend. Kissing another man while they had agreed to be "dating" each other was bad.

"I have another mess on my hands. I shouldn't have kissed you." Brisa scrubbed both hands down her face. "I apologize. I'll talk to Reggie about it and..." Why couldn't she figure out words to end her sentences anymore?

"Tell Thea I said goodbye." Brisa hurried down the steps before he could argue with her any more. She needed some time to flesh out her sentences. To do that, she needed to think.

And obviously, to think clearly, she needed to put space between herself and Wade.

She didn't check over her shoulder as she hurried down the sidewalk, but she was sure he watched her go.

CHAPTER SIXTEEN

THE THIRD TIME Wade opened the refrigerator door on Saturday night, he realized what he was searching for.

Beer. He wanted to find a cold beer in his nearly empty refrigerator.

He'd dropped Thea off for an end-of-the-summer slumber party at five o'clock, and since then, he'd been at loose ends.

"You should go to bed," he muttered to himself as he grabbed a bottle of water from the door and slammed the refrigerator closed. "Again." His first try had ended in aimless channel surfing until he'd decided he should make productive use of his time.

When he went back to work, he was going to have to make choices for health, dental and life insurance as well as at least ten different add-ons that were optional and sometimes expensive. Identifying what he needed and what holes were left in his military retirement benefits was almost as easy as assembling a thousand-piece jigsaw puzzle.

There were fewer pieces, but none of them fit together.

So, he'd tried the refrigerator. No luck.

"Good thing you didn't listen to that annoying voice that tried to convince you having a six-pack in the fridge for guests was only hospitality." Wade pressed his forehead against the cool stainless steel and wrinkled his nose against the to-scale drawing of Thea's bedroom.

His hope that Thea might get homesick had evaporated when she'd climbed out of his car, her backpack on one shoulder and the mermaid sleeping bag rolled up, shiny side out, under the other. She'd been nervous until another little girl had run up to the car and shouted, "Mermaids. I love mermaids!"

Thea had blinked but then said, "Me, too!" The high-pitched tones would drive Wade up the wall. Then she'd added, "My daddy has a pool. Want to come swimming sometime?" When the other little girl nodded until he was afraid her head would fall off, he realized he was going to have to adjust to those tones. Quickly.

"See you, Dad. Noon tomorrow. Don't forget." She waited for his promise before asking, "You're going to be okay, aren't you?" Two small lines appeared on her forehead. "I should have a cell phone so you can call me if you need me."

Wade had to laugh. It was a good try. They'd had this conversation the first night she'd stayed with him and it had come up a few more times since. Thea knew she wasn't old enough for her own phone.

Wade had listened to his ex-wife list the dangers of such a phone in this day and age when he'd opened the conversational can of worms. To Thea, he'd said, "I've researched options without internet access. When your mother gets home and has caught her breath, I'll talk to her." He'd put on protective padding first. Vanessa had been fiery in her conviction that Thea was still a kid and kids didn't need cell phones, not even smart girls like theirs. Not even for emergencies, which had always been Thea's sales pitch. "Until then, you have my number. You call me if you want to tonight. I'll be happy to come get you."

Her snort would have been cute if it hadn't been so disappointing.

"Brisa gave me some advice. She's smart. I've got this. I'll be fine." She dropped her stuff on the sidewalk and lunged across the passenger seat to throw her arms around his neck and kiss his cheek. "I will miss you, though. Don't cry."

Wade squeezed her tightly. "Let me walk you to the door. I should say hello to Isabel's mom and…"

Thea stepped back, a scowl wrinkling her forehead this time. "I'm not a baby. Mom knows Isabel's mom. It's okay. I can handle this." Then she'd slipped away quickly, slammed the door and picked up her stuff in a running swoop before trotting up to the front door with the other little girl. Thea was waving as it opened, and he got the impression that she would stand there and wave until it became awkward. If he was in the driveway, she would wait and wave.

Wade could still remember the sinking feeling as he'd driven away.

And the rest of the night? So much nothing.

It was too bad he and Mira had fizzled.

He could be racking his brain to build a second date as special as their first.

That reminded him of Brisa, and he wanted to do anything but think of her. How she'd hurried away after their kiss had been replayed in his mind too many times.

Then he remembered Mira's invitation to join the group at the pool.

"This is not a problem you need help with," he muttered and realized he'd done a lot of talking to himself over the long evening, as well. "Go to bed already." Wade stomped up the stairs to his bedroom and turned in a slow circle, his hands propped on his hips. His comforter was balled up on the floor and his sheets had clearly lost a battle. His first attempt at sleeping had been a failure.

"Fine. Go talk to people instead of yourself." He grabbed his T-shirt off the floor, slipped it over his head and hurried back down the stairs before he could talk himself out of going.

He didn't have to bare his pitiful problems. Listening to others talk would be enough to get him out of his head.

As he rounded the corner to the pool area, he could hear low murmurs. Some of his concern disappeared. This had been his final option to distract himself from how easy a cold beer would be right now. Then he heard the clink of a glass bottle.

Before he could fade back into the shadows and escape, Mira spotted him. "Drink up, boys. We're going to change over to water tonight."

"No, don't do that," Wade said as he squeezed his nape, the creeping anxiety immediately tightening the muscles. "It's fine. I won't stay for long." There. He could meet everyone and lock himself in his house until daylight. Sunrise would make things simpler.

"Come. Sit." Mira pointed at a chair before handing out bottles of water. "These men need to hydrate before our morning run, anyway. I went easy today since I had a date to get ready for." She met his stare and then tapped the seat next to hers. "We'll have to run twice as far tomorrow."

Sean immediately hushed the wave of

groans. "Shh! Reyna might not oversee Concord Court anymore, but I still follow her orders. We aren't supposed to even be here."

"You weren't so big on the rules before you were in looooooove," the guy opposite from Wade drawled. Then he raised a bottle. "Jason Ward, nice to meet you."

"Peter Kim, Marcus Bryant," Mira said as she pointed out the other vets, "and you already know Sean. Jason's right. The rules don't matter as much since ol' Sean doesn't have to worry about his boss and his job, now that Reyna is so much more..." The chuckles muffled her next words, but it was clear they'd covered this ground before.

"Wade's met Reyna. He gets it." Sean tipped his bottle back and drank. "Besides, you're just jealous. And Reyna makes a few rules worth it." Then he grinned. "Love is definitely worth it, amiright, Ward?"

Jason nodded slowly and firmly. "Yes, it makes everything worth it."

Wade unscrewed the cap as he waited for the conversation to pick up again.

"You gonna tell us anything about this date or no?" Marcus Bryant asked. "Some of us have to live through our friends because we got no time for blind dates." Then he motioned around the table. "And by some of us, I mean me. The rest of y'all are doing fine." He shook his head sadly.

Mira patted his shoulder. "Only made a new friend." Then she pointed at Wade. "This was my date."

The silence around the table was funny, but no one laughed out loud. In the shadows it was hard to read their expressions. That might have wounded his ego a bit if he hadn't known about her secret husband.

"What went wrong?" Sean asked innocently. Wade had a hunch Sean had already determined he and Mira might not be the perfect match that Brisa and Reyna had hoped for. That raised the question of why Sean had made the suggestion in the first place.

"Nothing. I had a blast. Marcus, if you ever find the girl you want to slow down for, Brisa can connect you to the most original date in Miami. We rode bikes. We saw art. We *made* art. It was a great way to meet someone new." Then she shook her finger at Peter. "You, I don't know if even

Brisa can find something you haven't already tried as far as dates go, but she's very good."

"Hey, I have a system," Peter said smoothly. "It works fine."

"Then why are you always single?" Marcus fired back. He and Peter traded fake mean glares before they turned back to the table. "Truth hurts, friend."

"Yeah," Peter murmured, "moving along, please."

Mira shook her head. "I'd tell these two to pretend to be nice and reasonable since it's your first night, Wade, but they can't manage it. Quiet is all we can hope for."

Wade laughed. Quietly. "It's like I'm back on a ship, but with more room to move around. I can handle it."

"Navy?" Marcus asked.

"Yes. Surgeon. I'm taking a job here at the hospital nearby." Wade sipped his water. "My daughter and I just moved in. You will see us at the pool if Thea has any say in the matter." That brought up the image of Brisa smiling as Thea practiced her sculls in the shallow end. That wasn't what he wanted.

"Other family here?" Peter asked.

Wade considered the question. Dodging it to avoid the usual reaction was his first impulse, but he wanted something better here. "Not really. My mom died a long time ago. I grew up in foster care, then the United States military became my family." Wade shrugged to show it was fine. It was always fine because what other choice did he have?

"You found a good place here," Marcus said and pretended to give him a high five. They were too far across from each other to reach. "Family like the Navy but with fewer restrictions."

Wade nodded. He expected Marcus was correct. They went around the table to tell what branch they'd served in, places they'd been stationed and the worst job they'd ever done in the service to their country. Wade was surprised when even Sean joined in.

"Okay, the social requirements are out of the way. Tell us about how this date fizzled," Sean said as he propped his chin on his hand, clearly all ears.

"Let it go, Wakefield," Mira said. "It was nice. Fun. We don't have a romantic connection." She wrinkled her nose at him. "I wanted to kiss him as much as I want to kiss you, which is to say, not at all."

"Ouch," Wade muttered as everyone at the table chuckled.

Mira patted his shoulder. "It's okay. I know the decision was mutual."

Sean scooted back in his chair. "Interesting. Almost as if you might have feelings for someone else already." He tapped his lips as if he was trying to come up with a name.

The way Mira stiffened beside him convinced Wade she was afraid Sean meant her, *her* feelings for someone else. Her fingers were wrapped tightly around the arm of her chair, as if she was ready to force herself to spill her secret.

"You could be right. I would have said no before this afternoon, though, so I didn't know I had *feelings* for someone else when I asked Brisa to set me up on a date." Wade sighed and unclenched Mira's fingers from the chair. "If I'd met Mira first, that might have been different."

Mira cleared her throat. "Nah. There's still the kissing thing. No desire." Her eyes met his as everyone laughed. It was difficult to see her face well, but he read gratitude there. He'd taken the bullet so she could work out how to tell them her secret on her own time.

Maybe he'd learned that from Brisa.

"Who's the lucky girl?" Sean asked.

"Drop it, Wakefield. It's his first visit. Give him a chance to settle in before I have to stop him from killing you for being so irritating," Mira said.

Sean held up both hands. "Fine. If he didn't come out here for advice, he didn't. I'll drop it." Sean watched him across the table, almost patiently.

"Did you know I was headed there? Possibly falling for someone else on Friday night, just before you suggested Mira?" Wade asked, one corner of his mouth curled as Sean's eyebrows shot up.

"The Monteros, man, they get in your blood," Sean said, knowingly. "I tried to warn you, but I was pretty sure it was already too late for you. First time I met Brisa, it was as if sunshine had taken human form. She's warm and friendly and…" Sean stopped. "She's not as confident as she acts."

"But you didn't fall for Brisa?" Wade rested his elbows on his knees. He'd already given up Reyna to Sean Wakefield. Was the guy secretly in love with Brisa, too?

"Nah, she's too much like me. We're fun. We're light. We're always happy, even when we're not. No way would we ever figure out life together." Sean sipped his water.

Wade grunted. Sean's answer was close to what Brisa had said on the rooftop of the Sandpiper hotel, the difference between the kind of men she and Reyna needed.

"You are definitely not that." Sean drank more water and waited for Wade's reaction.

He grunted again. It was true but he wasn't going to admit it.

"People like Brisa and me, we float." Sean held up a hand to imitate an easy, rolling wave. "We'd eventually float apart. What we need is an anchor, something that holds firm against the waves. You're a boat guy, Mr. Navy. You get that, right?"

Wade frowned as he considered that. An

anchor. Ties that would hold solidly against the waves.

Instead of weighing someone like Brisa down, an anchor would mean she could rest.

That's what he believed a family was. That was what he'd wanted his whole life.

Sean was saying Brisa needed the same thing, but Wade could be the anchor.

"That is one deep metaphor, Wakefield. All this time, you pretended you only understood bad poetry, yet here you are, painting pictures," Jason Ward drawled. "Wait until I tell Angela about this. You'll confirm every hope and dream in my professor's teaching life."

"Still need to nail the rhyme scheme, though," Peter added and ducked as Sean tossed his bottle cap at his head.

"Boys, no throwing things," Mira said firmly. "Do not make me pull out my soon-to-be teacher's voice, 'mkay?"

Mira had suggested this meeting as an informal group therapy session, but it was unlike any group Wade had been a part of. These were true friends, the kind that became family.

Looking in from the outside, he'd always assumed that trust born of bonds that couldn't be broken because they were built in shared history was the main selling point of a family. Going through the world with only himself to fully rely on meant he wanted that connection. He'd do anything to build it for Thea. The anchor image made perfect sense.

The only way he knew how to build that trust was to give it first. If trusting this group was a mistake, he'd know soon enough. "Say a man like me, who is not sunshine and rainbows or whatever Wakefield said, met a woman who needs that anchor. How would he convince her to dump her wealthy, handsome, superstar boyfriend and the life she's always lived to settle down with an alcoholic divorced father of one who will work terrible hours and spend a lot of time battling anxiety and the stress of a job he's meant to do?"

Wade slumped back in his chair, covered his face and muttered, "Man, I need a beer right now." It had taken everything in him to be honest with himself and this group around the table. They were sympathetic, yes. They understood so much of his struggle, yes.

But none of them lived inside his head, the one with an alarm ringing so loudly because he'd laid his emotions out like a huge target, ready for arrows.

Mira squeezed his shoulder. "It gets easier, trust me." Then she sighed. "But who am I to talk." She held up both hands. "I'm about to share something. We aren't talking about it tonight or until I say we are." She waited until everyone at the table nodded. It took a minute because it was clear they were dying to know, and none of them were good at keeping their opinions to themselves. When she was satisfied, she said, "I'm…married." She paused and waited for the men around the table to react.

None of them did. Wade relaxed in his chair. They'd promised her and they were keeping to it.

His trust was in good people.

"We've been separated longer than we were together and at some point, I'll get around to filing the papers. He's not a part of my life anymore. It's just a…thing."

Mira tangled her fingers together and stared hard at them.

Still, no one spoke.

Wade admired her bravery. He was also impressed at the self-control around the table.

"So, what are we going to do about Mc-Nally's romance?" Sean asked. He cleared his throat. "We're good at solving problems."

Wade pressed his hands on top of Mira's to tell her to relax the hard knot. When she nodded, he said, "Not much to be done while that boyfriend's in the picture. I certainly can't compete with Reggie Beaumont."

Some of his hope faded when every man around the table shook his head slowly, regretfully. That was a fact none of them could argue.

"Could we find another woman for Reggie? He gets a lot of publicity for dating gorgeous society types. Anybody know a woman more beautiful than Brisa?" Peter asked.

Then the guy laughed as if it was the funniest joke in the world.

Wade sighed.

Because it was funny.

"Okay, so Brisa has to make the decision," Mira said, "and to choose Wade, all he has to do is give her something Reggie doesn't. What are your secret weapons?"

Wade stared at her as if she'd lost her mind. "Secret weapons? No man who has anything that might attract a woman keeps that a secret?" He glanced around the table to find every man nodding in agreement. "I don't know how I managed to get my first wife. I've always been terrible at understanding women, if they're interested, why they're interested." He frowned. "Is my secret weapon being the worst, just so bad that someone kindhearted eventually picks me up and dusts me off?" He replayed the numerous ways in which Brisa had done exactly that. "Because if that works, I will totally lean into it. Stop feeding myself. Grow a hermit beard. Whatever."

Mira picked up her empty water bottle and examined it. "This is going to take a while, isn't it? With Ward, all we had to do was convince him to get over himself. And Wakefield had to be convinced he was worthy of a woman like Reyna. You…" She narrowed her eyes as she studied Wade. "It's sort of the same as Sean's problem with Reyna, except you have to accept the past and who you are now."

"And get rid of the celebrity boyfriend," Peter added in case they'd forgotten.

Mira cut him a mean frown. "Yes, Peter, we've got that." She turned back to Wade. "Secret weapons. You're different than the men Brisa has dated. That's the flip side of celebrity, in case you were wondering. And then there's Thea."

Wade smiled slowly. "Brisa loves Thea, like enjoys spending time with her to the point that she was practicing synchronized swimming moves in the pool with her." That had to be a secret weapon.

Mira's grin mirrored his. "Nobody and no problem can defeat this group, Wade McNally. We found the key to your win, right there. Brisa doesn't strike me as one of those people who fawns over every baby or toddler in sight. But she likes your kid, no question."

"The guy's not going to use his daughter to get a woman," Marcus said, then halted. "Or will he?"

"It's not using. It's…" Mira paused as she considered. "Wade is showing Brisa what his life is like. It's different because of Thea."

"And Thea, thanks to my ex-wife's encouragement, would be fully on board with this plan. They both think Brisa is a winner." Wade cleared his throat. "They're both smarter than I am, clearly."

Sean held his plastic water bottle up to the center of the table. The other guys stretched forward to clink their bottles against his. Wade and Mira followed suit. "To the intelligence of women. Where would we be without it?"

CHAPTER SEVENTEEN

ON MONDAY AFTERNOON, Brisa searched for her compact in her desk drawer. She needed to check her makeup. Her father's appointment was in thirty minutes, and she still hadn't determined the best way to explain to him that the grant rejections she'd gotten the week before were to be expected. Not every proposal was going to get a yes. That was the way of the world. The two of them as seasoned business people should understand that, of course.

Delivering that story confidently was going to take solid armor, flawless hair and makeup. Possibly high heels, but she didn't have time to go home and get any, so she'd have to make do with her cute ballet flats.

When she reached for a pen to make herself a note to bring a pair of heels to leave in her desk for emergencies, Brisa found the compact open. As she looked down, she realized her face was naked. In her sleepless fog, she hadn't put on any makeup that morning before she left the house. She was as nature made her.

Brisa blinked slowly as she came to terms with the fact that she'd never once asked herself, *Are you fully dressed?* that entire day. A sleepless Saturday night had bled into a restless Sunday. She'd managed to make the grueling run Mira put them through that morning, but after that, after the long shower and eating everything in her refrigerator, she'd been unable to focus on any one thing. Normally, half-finished projects annoyed her until they were complete.

Apparently, she was growing out of that trait. She had half a load of laundry folded, half a grocery list for the trip she'd intended to make but never had and half a book read that she couldn't remember.

One kiss. That's all it had taken to ruin her concentration.

And now, she was going to go up against her father with a couple of failures under her belt with a naked face.

"You okay, boss?" Sean asked as he

waved a hand in front of her eyes. "You've been staring at that same page for twenty minutes."

When he tapped the open binder on her desk, Brisa jerked as if she was coming awake again.

"Brainstorming," she answered, "but quietly. More of a gentle spring mist."

Sean raised his eyebrows, but he didn't argue. "Again, I ask, is everything okay?" He held up his phone. "Do I need to call Reyna?"

"Of course not," Brisa snapped. "You don't need to call her every time there's a problem."

"You aren't your usual self." Sean slid his phone into his pocket. "Let me know if I can help."

Brisa huffed out a loud breath that combined with a grumble. "I'm sorry. You're right. I'm not my usual self and it's irritating. That's all."

Sean gazed longingly at his office next door, as if he were dreaming of an easy escape.

"Listen, I only now…" She checked the clock she'd hung on the lobby wall one day when there was no one around to stop her from decorating as she liked. "After two o'clock in the afternoon, I have realized I forgot to put on makeup this morning. No mascara. No blush. Not even a lip balm." Brisa rested her head in her hands. "Is this the face of a woman in crisis or what?"

When he didn't answer, she raised her head. Sean pointed at his pocket. "Are you sure I shouldn't call your sister? I am not equipped for this conversation."

When she slumped against her chair, he said, "If it makes you feel any better, I didn't even notice. I thought you were sleepy, maybe tired or sick."

Brisa rolled her eyes. "Yes, those are the reasons many women put on makeup."

He pretended to write down a note on his hand. "Got it."

"My dad will be here any minute. Need my game face." She ran her fingers through her hair before pulling it up into a quick knot.

"You could impress him by doing that. I don't get how women just…" He mimed a twisting motion and then plopped his hands on his head.

Brisa straightened her shoulders. "It's my father. No one rattles me like he does. Now that I have to give him bad news about those grants…" When she'd tried to distract herself from the memory of this meeting over the weekend, she'd fallen headfirst into remembering Wade's kiss. Then, to drag herself out of that quicksand, she'd stepped right back into her work dilemma.

Reggie hadn't answered her calls, which might have been a blessing because she hadn't figured out what to say to him about the kiss yet, either.

Swimming in quicksand was even harder than synchronized swimming sculls.

"What can I do? We could lock the door, turn off the lights and pretend no one's home?" Sean asked as the reflection of sunlight moved across the wall. Someone had parked in front of the office.

Her father had landed.

"No time. The only way out is through," Brisa muttered. "Thanks for the pep talk, Sean. You don't make enough money for all you do around here."

"Good thing I love my job, then." They both turned as the lobby door opened.

When Reggie walked in, Brisa had the slow-motion effect of watching her life flash before her eyes. All she could hear was static in her brain as Sean greeted Reggie and they shook hands. She managed to nod at whatever Sean said as he left the office to give them some privacy and tilted her cheek up for Reggie's kiss.

After he plopped down in the chair opposite her, Brisa lost track of what happened until he waved his hand in front of her face. "Hello? Anybody home? You okay?"

Brisa blinked, restarted her brain. "Sorry. Long day." The ding of her phone snagged her attention and she picked it up.

Last minute phone call has come up. I'll come by Friday instead, no need for the weekly report that way. Confirm the details with Trina. Dad

For some reason, her father had loosened his probationary requirement and given her a few extra days' grace. That seemed... big. Was he going to try trusting her a little? Her father sometimes signed his texts with "Dad" as if she didn't have him in her phone and might not recognize who was sending the communication.

It was cute, but today she was instantly relieved by the reprieve.

"Looks like it's been a couple of long days." He touched under his eyes to point out her dark circles. Brisa didn't need his clarification or appreciate it. "I got your messages, but I was planning to drop in to see you." Reggie held out both arms as if he was saying, *And here I am.*

Telling him that she'd kissed Wade and wanted to find a way to end her setup with Reggie in order to… She had no idea what would come next, if it was something with Wade or running away to a deserted island where no one had ever heard of Reggie, Wade or men at all.

They were trouble. All of them. And they got her into trouble.

Brisa knew she needed to tell Reggie all her mixed-up emotions and come clean. It had seemed impossible over the phone, but when he reached into his pocket to pull out a ring box, breathing became the real challenge.

Then the door to the office opened again, and Wade and Thea walked in.

Meanwhile, Reggie popped the box open to reveal the largest diamond Brisa had ever seen.

Of the three adults in the room, Wade responded first. "Sorry. You're busy. We can come back."

"Excuse me, sir," Thea said as she marched up to the desk. Brisa didn't speak but she could see the wild urge to grab his daughter and run flash across Wade's face. Innocent Thea had no idea what a powder keg she was dancing on. "I need to tell my friend Brisa something, and then you can get back to business." Thea moved around the desk and wrapped her arms around Brisa's neck.

That was enough to get the hamster back on the wheel in Brisa's brain, so she inhaled deeply. Little girl. Suntan lotion. Reggie's expensive cologne.

And Wade watching it all.

"Isabel wants to be a mermaid, so we're going to start practicing together." Thea stepped back. Brisa frowned as she tried to assemble all the pieces quickly: Isabel,

Thea's friend from school who might like fish, and the sleepover where Thea wanted to make friends. Brisa's suggestion of pool time had sparked something. "When Isabel's not here, I'll coach you on your sculls, but she and I are developing our own routine." The patience and sadness on her face indicated Thea knew she was delivering the death knell to Brisa's synchronized swimming career.

"I'm glad to hear it. You'll both make excellent mermaids, I'm sure." Brisa turned Thea around and took out the weird ponytail that was listing sideways. She quickly gathered Thea's hair and twisted it into a messy bun to match her own. "Let me know when practice is. I need the inspiration."

Thea nodded and held her hand up for a high five.

Then Brisa realized there was no easy way out of this nightmare. "Reggie, this is Wade McNally. He's the new trauma surgeon at the hospital. Wade, this is Reggie Beaumont." No other introduction necessary. Wade had asked for an intro. She was sure he definitely hadn't expected it to be like this, though.

Reggie stood to give Wade a handshake. He tried to make conversation he usually used with fans, but Wade's monosyllabic answers weren't much help. Wade's eyes were locked on the ring box sitting square in the middle of Brisa's desk.

For good reason. Brisa glanced at it out of the corner of her eye the way she would a dangerous animal. No direct eye contact it could take as a challenge to leap for her throat.

"Thea, Brisa's busy. We'll drop in another day this week." Wade put his hands on his daughter's shoulders and walked her toward the door. The way Thea turned her head to watch Brisa as they went suggested Thea had picked up on something, but she wasn't sure where the tension was coming from.

Which was for the best. If she understood that Reggie was the unserious boyfriend who was about to make things a lot more serious, Thea would have had something to say. It would have been outrageous. And the whole building might have exploded.

Wade didn't look back.

When they were gone, Reggie said, "Cute kid. I didn't know you were into kids."

That's because she wasn't. Or she hadn't been.

"I've been helping them adjust to the move into Concord Court." Brisa waved her hand and ignored the hard knot in her stomach that formed as she said it.

Reggie watched her but eventually he accepted her answer. He pointed at the ring. "Try it on."

Brisa put her hand over the box but shook her head. "We need to talk about this first."

He braced his elbows on his knees. "Okay, but there are reporters outside who are going to be anxious to get a photo of the ring. This morning, management offered me three more years to play and one year to try assistant coaching. They're this close to giving it all to me. I need that ten-year commitment. Can't quit before I cross the finish line." He shrugged. "I drove from the stadium downtown to find the prettiest ring I could. We'll get 'engaged—'" he made air quotes around the word "—for a month or two and then realize how much happier we are as friends. Plenty of time to get the contract I want." He brushed his hands together. It was all decided in his mind.

Brisa hadn't expected to have to make a decision like this today. Maybe it was for the best that she was suddenly so tired that it was impossible to tie herself up in knots trying to find a way to make sure everyone was happy.

Everyone except her, anyway.

She closed the lid on the ring box and turned it in circles as she worked through answers in her head.

Without looking up, she said, "I kissed someone this weekend, Reggie. I was calling to tell you that."

When he didn't immediately answer, she looked up. He was frowning down at the crease in his linen pants. "Did anyone see you?"

Brisa slumped against her chair as at least three different answers flashed through her mind. "No." Every one of the answers started that way. Whatever it meant to her, Reggie was only concerned with his image. "But don't you see that…" How could she explain to him what that kiss meant when she wasn't sure herself?

"Then this plan could still work." Reggie moved closer and wrapped his hand around hers. "I'm so close, Brisa. Help me make it to the finish line."

She wanted to. For a lifetime, Brisa had done her best never to let down a friend. Whether it was money or time or influence or physical support, she'd shown up. This time felt different.

"Don't you want something real, Reggie? A real love?" Brisa asked. This was the question that scared her the most. The old Brisa would have laughed it off, refused to meet it head-on. This Brisa was too tired to keep dancing around the scary part.

"Yeah, but…" He licked his lips as he thought. "I'm going to take what I can get, I guess." He shook his head. "Finding real in this world, the way we move, Brisa, it's just…" He met her stare.

They both understood what he meant.

"What if I've found it? Would you want me to jeopardize that for this engagement?"

Brisa held his hand when he would have moved away. "Answer as my friend, not the guy with the long-term plan and team management right where he wants them."

Reggie gave a soft smile. "You had to go there. Play the friend card, didn't you?"

Brisa laughed. "Real friends are about as hard to find as real love, Reggie. I hope we are real friends, at least." She knew they were. She'd never laid herself open for another friend this way, but she had faith that Reggie would not disappoint her. He was Miami's sweetheart for a reason.

He held up one finger. "You might want to hold off on that. Now I have a confession to make." He grimaced. "The story is already out. I made a big show of walking out of the jewelry store with the box. Stopped at my car. Tossed it up in the air. When the paparazzi demanded to know what was inside and who it was for, I did my thing." He showed her his wink and point and held his arms out. There would be a dozen different photos of similar poses in the media by this afternoon. "If there aren't people in the parking lot right now ready for a shot of you with a diamond on your finger, I'll be shocked."

Brisa slumped forward onto her desk. Her brain needed support and she was too tired to hold her head up anymore.

It would be so easy to lose her temper, to blast Reggie about pushing their agreement and letting her down and a million other hurts that boiled up from past friends and bad decisions. His hands covered hers as he said, "I'm sorry. I should have gotten your okay first. I assumed… You've been ready for every other thing, I just…" He sighed. "I messed up."

Brisa realized she'd reached the level of self-awareness that allowed her to understand Reggie was in the spot she'd so often put herself in. He'd made a mistake. It was about to cause a mess.

And there was no way out of the mess but through it.

How could she be angry at him for doing what she'd done over and over until people expected it of her?

Brisa sat up straight. "It would be so much easier for us both if I slip the ring on and we go pose for photos." Easy was so tempting at that point. If she bought some time, she'd be able to explain things to Wade and to her family. The Monteros would never approve, but that would be a problem for another day and one with an eventual solution, even if a fake engagement reinforced their view of her, the one she was slowly changing.

"Easy, yeah, but…" Reggie shook his head. "If you've found something real, we're going to have to do this the hard way. I wouldn't gamble real love on anything, not even a ten-year contract to coach in my home stadium."

His eyes were warm as he smiled at her. "Especially not when it involves one of the only people in the world I'd call a real friend." He clapped his hands. "So, what do we do? How do we handle this?" Reggie Beaumont moved quickly, on and off the field.

Brisa rubbed her eyes. "We could get engaged today and you could be seen kissing another woman in a bar tonight." He didn't answer. "No one would believe it of you. Some other poor woman would be trashed for tempting Miami's favorite boy."

No matter how she plotted, Brisa couldn't come up with any other answer except the truth. "You asked. I said no. We're better as friends than married. It's the only way to go."

"Then you handle the fallout, right? You'll be the one who broke my heart." Reggie squeezed his eyes shut. "I made a big mistake."

Brisa had to laugh. She had to. There was no other option.

Getting caught up in her own clever plan, the one she'd crafted to throw her father off, was so on brand for Brisa Montero that it was hilarious. She was as guilty of using Montero maneuvers as her father, especially when she added in the fact that she'd tried to set her sister up against her will. That was exactly what Reggie had protected Brisa from: her father's unappreciated matchmaking.

When she realized her giggles were scaring Reggie, she sucked in a breath and waved her hands. "I'm fine. I'm fine. Really."

He wasn't convinced.

When she could talk without gasping,

Brisa said, "You know those cartoons where a character doesn't understand how boomerangs work? Some bear throws one and then gets knocked out when it comes back around? That is a visual representation of my life right now. It's so funny."

She wiped under both eyes and tried to catch her breath.

"I'm not leaving you alone in here like this. Let's call your sister." Reggie held his hand out. He wanted her phone to make the call for reinforcements.

The last thing Brisa wanted was her sister riding to her rescue.

"No. Paste on a brokenhearted face, go outside and tell everyone you asked but that I couldn't risk my best friendship in the world on something as risky as marriage. Make a joke or something. Get in your car and leave, taking as many of the guys following you as you can." Brisa nodded. "The truth. That's what we're going with."

Reggie stood and asked, "What are you going to tell the guy? I'm assuming it was the one with the cute daughter whose hair you twisted up as if you've done it every

morning before sending her off to school…
or maybe you *will* do that, eventually."

Brisa's lips twitched. "I'm going to tell
him the truth, too. When the interest in
your broken heart dies down a bit, I'll tell
him. I don't want him or his cute daughter caught up in the paparazzi cross fire.
They'll be looking for my take on the story,
too. Wade would not be happy if Thea's
face made it onto the gossip sites."

"We don't want Wade to be unhappy,"
Reggie said.

"I really don't," Brisa agreed.

His slow smile was beautiful. Reggie
Beaumont could charm anyone with that
smile. "You want to leave first? I might be
able to draw them off you."

Brisa shook her head. "I'm going to wait.
Eventually, the crowd will disappear. I
need a full face of makeup before I go out
to pose for photos."

Reggie frowned. "I knew something was
different about you. Are you sick?"

Brisa huffed out a laugh. Men really paid
zero attention to the little things. "I was,
but I'm better. Stronger."

He came around the desk to press a kiss

to her forehead. "If the surgeon gives you trouble, let me know." Then he straightened his jacket and stepped around the desk to march toward the door.

"Hey, Reggie," Brisa called, "don't quit before you cross the finish line. Let me know if there's anything I can do to help with your negotiations. As a Montero." Monteros had zero to do with Miami sports, but it was all she had to offer.

He nodded. "You bet. I know I can count on my friends." Then he waved and stepped outside. The door shut before she could hear any hoopla over his appearance. Brisa locked the door, even though the office didn't close for another hour. If Sean needed in, he could use his key.

Then she went back to her desk, lined up all her binders and stared at them.

She'd accomplished so much at Concord Court. Were there still challenges? Yes. She'd met other challenges, so she could do this, too.

Reggie's mess was beyond her control right now.

She had a meeting scheduled with her father at the end of the week.

With that reprieve, she could take the bad news about the rejected grant applications and turn it around with a positive follow-up, but what? More applications she'd sent out? That was one idea.

Except she still didn't know how to correctly construct her grant proposals. What she *didn't* need was more rejection.

To take her mind off the idea of having to run the gauntlet of Miami's gossip reporters on her way to her townhome, Brisa flipped through her program binders and eventually rested her head on the Shelter to Service binder, her favorite. Her first success had been with Julius Stewart, the man who owned one of the largest grocery distribution chains and dog food companies in the country. He'd funded Sean's Shelter to Service dog training program and offered his support for other things at Concord Court.

What if she'd been aiming too high to start out with the business lab idea?

That would surprise no one. Too high, too fast.

She leaned back and considered what she needed most to get the funding to support small business loans. All roads led back to money.

To get big money, she needed big grants.

To get big grants, she needed…help. Expertise. A grant writer? Was there such a thing? Where would she find one and how would she pay one?

To pay the grant writer, she needed… money, but a lot less than she'd aimed for to start with.

A small enough sum that someone like Julius Stewart might be persuaded to help. Could it be that easy to prove to her father that she was moving forward? Slowly. Intelligently. She could show a setback and a Plan B, a smaller step that put her on the right track.

At this point, she had no other options. Reporters were outside. She needed to try something to feel like herself, to know she'd actually taken steps forward. Turning down Reggie was a new Brisa thing to do. Following it up with determination in her career would be another new Brisa thing.

The urge to call or track down Wade and Thea was strong, but the smart thing would be to put some space between them and this Reggie update. She'd focus on Concord Court first. Being successful there would give her the confidence to lay everything out for Wade and wait for his decision.

When the news hit about breaking Reggie's heart, it would be nice to have real tangible proof that new Brisa was staying here at Concord Court. She picked up the phone and dialed Julius Stewart's office. She had to give this a try.

CHAPTER EIGHTEEN

ON FRIDAY MORNING, a new Brisa strode into the Concord Court lobby. Her sister was seated behind the desk, so it was twice as satisfying to watch Reyna immediately stand and move out of her way. She had business to conduct. Reyna supported that. Today, they were on the right track.

"There's my baby sister," Reyna said as she clapped. "Every single day, you've gotten stronger. If Dad doesn't recognize you've got this whole situation under control today, well..."

Brisa waited for Reyna to finish the sentence.

"We'll have to keep trying until next week." Reyna wrinkled her nose. "It was more powerful when I trailed off, almost like we had any other option than to keep working on him."

Brisa laughed. "I get it, Rey. I appreciate the support." She smoothed her hand down the tailored jacket she'd chosen. "Am I ready?"

Sean squinted as he did a slow turn around her. "Makeup appears to be on. Hair is brushed. You've cleared the hurdles that took you down on Monday."

Reyna shot him the patient stare she'd started using when he was being silly at the wrong time.

"I like the suit." Reyna motioned up and down. "Makes you seem…business-y."

"It should. It's awfully expensive." Brisa sighed as she put down the briefcase she'd purchased for her second meeting with Julius Stewart the day before. "This 'living on a paycheck' business is for the birds, but I'll figure out the credit card payments for the suit and briefcase when the bill comes."

She'd changed all the addresses on all the bills. Instead of her father's assistant opening them and paying them, Brisa was going to tackle that. Every day, she cringed when the mailman came.

It would take some time to get over flinching when she read the bottom line.

Her sister could read her thoughts.

"I'm buying lunch." Reyna smiled. "Every day next week."

Brisa tipped her chin up. "We'll actually go to brunch at the club on Sunday, so that's another meal. Those cards will be paid in no time."

Reyna squeezed her hard. "You don't have to do this alone, BB. I've got you."

Brisa blinked her eyes as she refused to let tears ruin her makeup. Not today. Today was the day she showed her father that she'd had a setback and she'd recovered. Without him. No mascara streak allowed.

"What time is your meeting?" Sean asked as he stepped up and hugged them both affectionately. "Ten o'clock." Brisa checked the clock. Plenty of time to clear off her desk.

Brisa slipped into her chair, immediately removed the heels she'd regretted choosing on the walk over and opened up her computer.

Then she realized Sean and Reyna had taken up residence in the chairs opposite her.

"What?" Brisa asked.

"We have something we'd like to discuss with you because we love you," Reyna said, her lips twitching. Whatever it was, she was enjoying it way too much. "You've been neglecting your training."

Brisa frowned as she checked her email. Nothing there. "Training for what?"

"A gold medal win?" Sean drawled. "How quickly you've forgotten. Thea's been out at the pool almost every day this week without you."

Brisa slumped back in her chair. Was there a rule somewhere that said when a woman had one area of her life going well, something else had to go off the rails?

"I'm giving Wade some distance until the press disappears, so I've postponed my training." Brisa ignored them. Eventually they'd go back to work, wouldn't they?

Sean tipped his chin up as if he was still waiting for more information.

"And I'm scared." Brisa shrugged. There was no sense in hiding it. "I've messed up so many times with him. So. Many. Times. He and Thea don't need to be caught up in Miami's fascination with Brisa Montero. It's like, how much forgiveness does one person have inside them? When things are quiet, I'll resume training. Maybe Wade will have restocked on second or third or fifth chances, whatever I'm on."

She tangled her fingers together and studied her nails as she tried to remember when was the last time she'd had a manicure. She picked at a hangnail and mourned pretty fingernails along with her delay at spending time with Wade.

"Does that look like she's feeling sorry for herself?" Sean asked.

"Impossible. Can't be done in that suit." Reyna sniffed. Her huge grin was irritating. "It's been long enough, Brisa."

Had it? Brisa wanted that to be true, but Reyna hadn't seen Wade's face as he'd stared at the engagement ring.

Her sister scooted forward. "What if he's not angry? What if he thinks your heart is broken instead?" Reyna asked. "What if he's on the totally wrong track because you haven't been honest with him? What if he's sure your engagement failed because he kissed you and Reggie got mad and he's secretly afraid he ruined your life?" Reyna raised her eyebrows. "You'd owe it to him to correct that thinking as quickly as you could, wouldn't you?"

Brisa fiddled with the cord to her mouse as she considered that. She'd been avoiding Wade because she was embarrassed or ashamed of making another mess. What if he thought it was worse than that? Then it wasn't about how many chances he'd given her. It was only about clearing up a misunderstanding.

Which she had decades of experience with.

"He promised to pay the next time we go to Surf and Turf. What if we lure him out there with the promise of food, and Sean and I conveniently forget to show up?" Reyna asked before she straightened. "No, we tell him to ride with us, that you're meeting us there, then we dump him and drive away. He'll have to listen to you then."

Sean frowned. "Isn't that kidnapping? I'm not down for jail time for your baby sister."

Brisa laughed as Reyna waited for him to meet her stare. "You won't go to jail for me?"

He rolled his eyes. "For you, yes. For

her…" He pointed at Brisa and then waved his hand as if it was a no-go.

Before she could convince her sister that jail time would not be required, her phone rang. Brisa checked the display to see her father's name. "Morning, Daddy… You need to reschedule? If coming here doesn't work, I can swing by your office. We have all hands on deck at Concord Court today." Brisa stuck her tongue out as she realized how grossly chipper she sounded. She wanted to get this over with as soon as possible. One big problem untangled would leave her plenty of time to deal with Wade.

And she wanted to get to dealing with Wade.

"Brisa, listen carefully. Is your sister with you?" her father asked. Brisa pressed the phone harder against her ear. It was difficult to understand him. There was road noise and something else in the background.

"Reyna? She's here. Do you need to talk to her?" Brisa asked. Why hadn't he called Reyna's phone if that was the case?

"No. Listen to me." He coughed. "I'm headed to the hospital by ambulance. There was an accident. I need you…" He coughed again and Brisa stood slowly, the alarm raising goose bumps on her arm.

"Daddy, are you okay?" she asked, before pressing her fingers to her mouth. Silly question. He was in an ambulance.

"I will be fine, Brisa. I promise. Do not worry. I need you or your sister to go and pick up Marisol to bring her here. She doesn't drive enough to be steady to make the trip in a hurry and…" He coughed again. "Please tell her about the accident and that I am fine. Do you understand? I do not want her to worry."

Reyna had picked up on the problem and moved to grip Brisa's arm tightly.

"I understand, Daddy. I'll go and get Marisol. Reyna will head to the emergency room to meet you. We'll take care of everything," Brisa said firmly and pinched her nose to prevent the tears from falling. Her father didn't need sobbing at this point.

"Thank you. Please drive carefully, baby. Both of you." Then he ended the call and Brisa frowned down at her phone.

"What is it?" Reyna asked.

"I think it's a car accident. It was hard to

understand, but Daddy's on the way to the hospital. He wants me to go and get Marisol." Brisa stared from her sister to Sean. "I'll go. Lock up the office and both of you go meet him in the emergency room. And you make sure you tell him he promised he'd be fine. I won't accept anything less. It would be un-Montero-like."

Sean pulled his keys out. "Got it, boss. We're on it."

Reyna let him pull her toward the door. "Should one of us stay..."

"Sean, get her in the truck and go," Brisa snapped and followed them out. As she raced to her townhome and her car, she experienced half a second of irritation at Reyna who wanted to keep the business going at a time like this and then let it all go as she slid behind the wheel of her convertible.

Drive carefully. That was her father's order. She was going to prove her Monteroness by following it. Before she turned out of the Concord Court driveway, she accessed the hands-free phone and pulled up Wade's number. She pressed it to call before she could even ask herself what she was doing.

"Brisa?" he answered on the first ring. As if he were anxious for her call. Not angry. Maybe. She'd think about that later.

"Wade, are you at the hospital by chance?" Brisa couldn't remember how soon his schedule started or when his ex-wife would be home so Thea might still be with him. All she was sure of was that she wanted Wade near her father and soon.

"I am, actually. Dr. Holt had a liver transplant scheduled. He asked me to observe. Since Vanessa and Steve made it home last night, I decided to…" He paused. "What's wrong?"

As she sped through a yellow light, Brisa forced herself to take her foot off the gas. *Drive carefully, baby.* That's what her father had said.

"My father is headed to Emergency. There was some kind of accident. I know we've had some…" How could she describe their relationship?

"I'll head down there now. Are you on your way?" His voice was firm. Certain. Reassuring. It was easier to drive slowly since Brisa immediately felt better because Wade would be nearby.

"I'm on my way to get my stepmother. Reyna and Sean will be there soon." Brisa inhaled slowly. They had a plan. Everything was better with a plan.

"We'll be here when you arrive. Slow down. He'll get the best care. You know that." Wade was calm.

And he was right.

"Thanks. I'll see you soon." She quit the call because she needed to concentrate, but she missed his voice as soon as she did.

Luckily, traffic was lighter than normal, and she turned into the long driveway to her parents' home without much trouble. Her car could almost operate on autopilot as she made the familiar trip.

Turning down the long driveway lined with old oaks and royal poinciana trees, she might as well have stepped back in time to when she was a little girl. The trees had shaded the Montero grounds then, and nothing had changed. Warm sunshine illuminated the paved area between the garages. As she drove through the portico, Brisa waved at the security camera that covered all entries and exits on the grounds. It was an old habit. She'd started doing it when she was successful in sneaking out of the house as a teenager. She slammed the door and decided to gamble that Marisol would be in her favorite spot on the planet, the covered lanai that overlooked the pool and the ocean.

"Brisa, what are you doing here?" Marisol asked as she set down her coffee cup. She was dressed for a lazy day at home, but Marisol Montero had impeccable fashion sense. Even for days at home, she was smartly dressed. "Is something wrong?"

Brisa forced herself to take a deep breath. Her father wanted Marisol not to worry. Most of that relied on Brisa's delivery. "Daddy called and asked me to come pick you up. He's had an accident, but he's fine." Brisa wrapped her arm around Marisol's shoulders as she stood. "He's fine. We talked on the phone. He didn't want you to have to fight the traffic, so he asked me to bring you to see him. He'll probably have to wait a bit, be checked out before he's released. He knew you would worry." There. It sounded so everyday when she said it like that. Marisol's eyes were locked to her face, so Brisa smiled. She'd had years of experience telling half-truths and white lies, so this should be no challenge.

Thanks to the knowledge that Reyna and Wade were both headed toward her father, it was easy for Brisa to be strong for Marisol.

"Let me grab my purse, and we'll go." Marisol glanced around as if she wasn't exactly sure where her purse lived.

"You know what? You don't even need it. I'll wait with you and bring you home when Daddy is released. We'll make him ride in the tiny back seat." She grinned at Marisol and wrapped her arm around her stepmother to help her down the stairs. Under normal circumstances, Marisol would float or dance down the stairs with style. Today, this close, with her confusion, Brisa understood that Marisol was as human as the rest of them. Even her father had succumbed to the world's imperfections today.

"Dan took the week off to go visit his mother," Marisol said quietly as she buckled her seat belt. "Your father has enjoyed driving himself everywhere and now this." She shook her head.

Her father, the man who worked every

single waking minute of every single day
and if you were late to dinner, ordered din-
ner for you, used a driver most of the time.
That explained one of Brisa's questions.
She'd been afraid to ask what happened to
Dan in the accident.

"Accidents happen. It's one of those
things," Brisa murmured as she negotiated
the traffic. It was easier to pretend everything was fine with that distraction.

"We were surprised you didn't tell us
about Reggie's proposal." Marisol stared
hard out the window. Was she urging Brisa
to go faster? Brisa pushed harder on the
gas pedal.

"I hope you haven't had to answer too
many questions at the club." Their complaints always revolved around the gossips
at the club and being caught without answers. "Reggie's ready to be married, but I
didn't think that was a good enough reason
to say yes."

Marisol sighed. "You two were never
a love match anyway." Then she patted
Brisa's arm. "Right?"

Brisa supposed it made perfect sense that
her father and stepmother had seen through

her careful plot to throw off matchmaking. They'd been untangling her messes as long as she had.

"Right. Friends, who made easy plus-ones to ward off matchmakers," Brisa said. They were quiet for the rest of the drive. Brisa parked in the deck instead of dropping her stepmother at the door. In case the situation was worse than she'd convinced herself it would be, Brisa needed to be on hand to support Marisol. That was the job she'd been assigned.

And it was good thinking on her father's part.

For some reason, the woman who knew the hospital backward and forward, thanks to years of fundraising and volunteer committees, was struggling to find the elevators. They hurried through the humid parking deck and into the hospital, where Brisa took control.

"This way, Mari," Brisa murmured and was happy when Marisol slipped a hand inside hers. This was the woman who'd kept her connected to the Montero family through some rough patches. It was sweet that Marisol depended on her when she needed to.

When they made it to the emergency lobby, Wade was standing outside the double doors. Her panic must have shown on her face, but he held up a hand. "I'm here to lead you back. He's going to be okay." His lips curled. It wasn't a full smile, but it warmed his eyes. Brisa would call him a friend in that moment, and she believed he would do the same for her.

As Marisol hurried ahead, Brisa said to Wade, "You don't have to wait with us, but I needed you here until I could make it myself."

Wade wrinkled his nose. "You better let me get you past the nurse in charge. She's a Reggie Beaumont superfan, according to her lanyard, so…" He held the doors open and waited for her to step inside. "Left corner, in the back."

Brisa gripped his hand as she followed his directions and joined her family around her father's bed. There was a lump on her father's head, his face was bruised as if his nose was broken, and he was surrounded by machinery. Brisa immediately turned to Wade for an explanation.

"He's going to be fine, Brisa. Pulmonary contusions caused by impact. The ER doctor's scheduled a chest X-ray and CT scan to be supersafe." Wade's voice was quiet. Eventually, her body settled, resting against his and she got control. "The bruises on his lungs will heal. They're monitoring his oxygen levels to see if oxygen therapy is called for. The ER doctor doesn't think anything's broken, which is amazing." Wade squeezed her hand tightly.

"I'm sorry. I was holding it together and then… I wasn't." Brisa forced herself to stand on her own, but Wade didn't let go.

"You did exactly what you needed to do."

Brisa realized half the staff in the ER and everyone gathered around her father's bed was watching them.

"McNally, you can release me, right? Send me home." Her father's voice was stronger than it had been on the phone, but he coughed at the end.

Brisa bit her lip to contain her smile as she stepped up next to her father. "McNally needs to go back to his office. We'll let the ER doctor make any decisions and we won't argue with him if you need to stay overnight, Daddy." She pressed her hands on the sheets next to her father and relaxed a fraction when he gripped her hand.

Marisol was frowning as fiercely as her father. "You will be staying here overnight. I insist."

"My oxygen levels are fine," her father said as he held up the finger with some kind of clamp on it. He shook it at the machine that showed numbers fluctuating in the eighties.

"What is a good number?" Brisa asked her sister under her breath. Wade chuckled quietly behind her.

"At least seventy, but a Montero number is closer to one hundred. That's the goal." Reyna wrapped her arm around Brisa's shoulder. "Good job, BB. They've been arguing since Marisol walked in, so you did exactly as you were ordered."

"Of course, I did. I would never disobey my father," she said with a straight face, but it was louder than she intended, and all other conversation stopped.

"Fine. I might disobey my father, but it's

more likely I'll use a little lie to get out of trouble." Brisa shook her head. Was she going to do this? "Are you on any painkillers by chance?"

Her father drawled, "My mind is clear. Very clear."

She nodded. Of course, it was. She stared over her shoulder at Wade in a weak attempt at making a wimpy apology and confessed, "Reggie and I had an arrangement to keep you from setting me up with eligible men you favored for me. The engagement? I was supposed to say yes, but I couldn't." She held out her hand to tick off the points. "I'm going to get all this off my chest here. I set up a personal ad for Reyna and corresponded with Wade McNally on her behalf until she went and fell for Sean. That's where the matchmaking thing started." Two fingers. She met her sister's stare. Instead of disappointment, Reyna just rolled her eyes. Wade squeezed her shoulder. "I received two grant rejections last week that I haven't told you about, Daddy, but I have a plan to fix that. I met with Julius Stewart, got a much smaller contribution that will allow me to hire a freelance grant writer who will get this small business lab's funding moving." Three fingers.

She wanted to clear the air completely, but she was forgetting something.

"I'm going to heal, it's okay, Brisa. Save some of this confessing for another day," her father whispered.

Brisa laughed and held up her fourth finger. "Wade McNally might not know it yet, but he's going to fall in love with me. I've been training for this my whole life and I will use every bit of Montero stubbornness and conniving to make it happen."

Sean muttered, "The guy's already so far gone he's about to come all the way back around and get you himself." Brisa didn't check on Wade's reaction to either her bold statement or Sean's comments. There would be time for that later.

"What else, daughter?" Her father pointed at the knot on his forehead. "I already have a headache. We might as well clear the air."

So she held out her hand to show him she was on her fifth point. "I want you to be proud of me. You. Reyna. Marisol. I want you all to be proud of me. That's it. The end. I might have tried to show you how little your disapproval hurt, but we're going to change the whole conversation. I'm going to make Concord Court work. I'm going to make my big ideas work. I'm a Montero. I won't stop until you're proud to call me a Montero, too."

Her father wrapped his hand around hers and pulled her to him. "I have always been proud of my beautiful girls. Always. Worried. You have worried me. Both of you. It's unacceptable. If you would both settle down here, follow my direction, then things would go much more smoothly for us all." He shook his head and grimaced. "You are on exactly the right track with Julius Stewart, the grant writer, Wade McNally, all of it. I had to drag you both here to get this going. I'm an old man. I wondered if you would both fight me to the end."

Brisa stared at her sister across the bed and they shared a smile.

"Safe. Secure. Home. Together. That's all I ask of you. From either one of you. Instead of demanding you be Monteros," he said slowly, "I will ask you to be Brisa and Reyna first." He lifted a shoulder in a careful shrug. "Let's see if that is any less successful."

Brisa was a little ticked off, and a lot relieved that her father was as Luis Montero as ever. His brilliant idea was to back off, something she and Reyna had been demanding since they could string words together.

And he was proud!

"Thank you for calling me, Daddy. I'm glad I had a chance to help." Brisa stared down at him and tried not to let the fear of his injuries and how much older he seemed in a hospital bed swamp her. Their way forward was going to be bumpy, but they were all going to go together.

"You're number two in my phone, Brisa. When I need help, only Marisol comes before you." He smiled.

Reyna muttered, "If she's number two, what number am I? Three?"

Her father shook his head. "Four. Sorry. You were a world away for so long and Trina has all my credit card information."

Brisa knew her eyes were huge as she watched her sister, her perfect sister's face, as she struggled to come to grips with the fact that their father would call his assistant before he called her. Eventually, Reyna said, "That's fair. Unexpected, but fair."

Sean wrapped his arms around her shoulders and pulled her back to lean against him. "You're number one on my speed dial." Everyone laughed and Brisa finally believed that everything was going to be okay.

Better than okay. Perfect.

"If you have any questions or need my help, call me. I'll be in my office for a bit, working on my benefit forms," Wade muttered, "but call me whenever. Anytime. For whatever you need. I mean it."

Sean drawled, "It sounds like you're busy, Doc."

Brisa intended to glare at Sean, but her sister already had it under control. "I want to walk out with you."

Wade tangled their fingers together and led her away. When they were in the ER lobby, Brisa asked, "Which Reggie Beaumont fan do I need to watch out for?"

Wade bent his head closer to hers to answer. "Short brunette. You'll find Reggie's jersey number on her lanyard, but maybe she's a Dr. Wade McNally fan. She smiled at me on the way out." His low voice raised the shiver again and Brisa couldn't stop it. Her eyes locked onto his.

"We need to talk, Dr. McNally. I have someone in mind for your second date, the one I owe you since Mira didn't work out." Brisa had every intention of being that second date. She'd stated her plan clearly. All Wade had to do was agree and surrender.

He tipped his head back and studied her face. "No more blind dates. I'm giving up on love. It'll just be me and my gold medal–winning astronaut daughter." His lips curled.

So he was going to be difficult. Fine. She deserved a little of that.

"Give it one more shot. Please. For me." Brisa raised her eyebrows. She knew a hundred different flirting tricks, but none of them were right for Wade.

"Okay, but I'm planning the date. I want it to be impressive, something that could convince this woman, the only one in the world who might be right for me, that I'm her match." Wade waited. "Do we have a deal?"

Brisa smiled and threw her arms around him. "I love a good negotiation. Count me in, Doc."

CHAPTER NINETEEN

WHEN WADE PARKED in front of The Amazing Space Race Escape, he glanced over at his daughter. Thea was still buckled in, but the urge to leap, run, slam, and all other things "Thea," was easy to read in her expression. He hoped this worked out the way it did in his head.

"Are you sure this is a good date idea?" he asked her as she unbuckled her belt. He'd liked his first suggestion better, returning to the bar at the top of the Sandpiper Hotel, but Thea and Vanessa had agreed with Mira and the rest of the pool group: Thea was his number one secret weapon in the war for Brisa's affection. No one else had another like her.

The Amazing Space Race Escape would display all of Thea's beauty perfectly.

"Dad, we've been over this," Thea said slowly. "Brisa likes me." And that was it.

That was the single most important argument any of them had made.

It was strong.

"Okay, let's work out how we're going to do this," he said. "What are we going to say to win her over?"

Thea paused as if to give the question serious study. "I'm going to remind her that she doesn't have a boyfriend anymore. You don't have a girlfriend." She held her hands out at both sides as if there was nothing else to add.

"You think that will do it?" Wade smiled as Thea shoved messy hair off her face. When he'd picked her up, Thea's hair had been in a neat ponytail. He suspected this change was another of Thea's tactics. Brisa did hair like it was second nature. Thea had a lot of hair. To remind her that he was also cool enough to attract a date sometimes, Wade held his hands out at his sides like Thea had.

"What are you doing?" she asked.

"Nothing." He checked the parking lot. Still no Brisa.

"Relax. You look nice. We know Brisa approves." Thea put her hand on his shoulder. He took that to mean reassurance. He could use reassurance. For some reason, this single date felt big. Really important. "I know Brisa will love this escape room. She enjoyed the planetarium, said it felt like she was flying through space. Here, we will be in a malfunctioning biodome racing against the clock to save our party from extinction." She clasped her hands together. "What could be more romantic than that?"

Candlelight. Satiny pink dresses. Silky warm skin. Bare feet in an empty glass-bottomed pool.

All those things made Wade's list ahead of escape room, but Brisa had turned into the parking lot.

"Don't mess this up, Dad. Brisa is pretty enough to have lots of choices, even if she really likes me." Thea met his stare to make sure he understood how important her advice was.

"Grab the flowers." Wade pointed at the back seat and opened his door.

By the time Thea made it out of the SUV to stand next to him, Brisa had parked and gotten out of her car. She stopped in front of them. "Surprise. I'm your date."

Wade smiled slowly. "Surprise. I know." He motioned at Thea to hand Brisa the flowers. "I brought my good luck charm."

He watched Thea wrap her arms around Brisa's waist and hoped they weren't making a huge, gigantic, child-crushing, heartbreaking mistake. A three-way love story between him, Brisa and Thea was dangerous, but there was no arguing that Brisa's smile brightened at whatever Thea had whispered in her ear.

"Hold these for me," Brisa said and turned Thea around. With some complicated, quick twist, she'd wrapped Thea's hair up into a functional bun, and then held her hand out for her flowers. "I need to teach you how to do that on your own."

"Or you could spend lots of time with me and do it yourself," Thea said as she rapidly fluttered her eyelashes.

"Thea, take this inside and pay for the escape room, please. The reservation is under our last name." Wade held out his credit card and shooed her toward the door.

A minute to talk to Brisa alone. He had to have one.

After Thea was inside, he said, "I asked Thea for help planning the kind of date that would convince a woman to fall in love. I should have been more specific." He crossed his arms over his chest and waited for Brisa to respond.

Her chuckle was sweet, but she stepped up beside him and pressed her lips against his. "Just needed one small improvement." She relaxed against him when he wrapped his arms around her waist to pull her close and Wade relaxed for the first time since he'd seen Reggie Beaumont with a ring box.

Brisa was here.

Brisa was here with him.

"If you need time to get over Beaumont, I understand. We can go as slowly as Thea will allow us," he said, content to stand forever on the sidewalk with her.

Brisa shrugged. "Reggie and I are friends. We were always only friends. He's as much a plotter as I am, so this is just the latest Brisa Montero mess that has to blow over, but my heart was never involved. I don't want it to splash all over you."

"That guy is not smart. At all. I'm glad." He smiled as she did.

"He never brought me to an escape room. I don't know how this works." Brisa pointed at a gnarly green alien who was clearly part of the reason people might want to escape.

"We're on a malfunctioning Mars bio-dome and we have only an hour to solve all the puzzles required to restore it or we will die a ghastly, oxygenless death. That's the main thrust of the story." Wade shook his head. "Thea's ghoulish excitement over dying on another planet took some adjustment this morning."

Brisa pressed her forehead against his shoulder as she laughed. "I bet. It's a good thing she's here. Thea told me I was too old to be an astronaut. Have they relaxed the rules?"

Too old? Stunned, Wade had to remember to close his mouth. He'd ask for details but that sounded so much like something Thea would say that he really didn't want to hear the ins and outs of that conversation. "I had to bring her. I'm not sure either one of us is smart enough to solve the puzzles and I don't want to die on Mars, not before I kiss you once or twice or a thousand times."

Brisa narrowed her eyes. "Are you sure? I have no military experience. I'm not a surgeon. Thea's great, but we still don't know if I like other children, kids who act their age. What about your ideal woman?"

Wade shook his head. "It's the weirdest thing. Your father helped me understand how wrong I was. You may or may not remember that I had this idea that I was going to prepare Thea so she'd never be as lost as I was when she grew up.

"She'd learn to budget properly. She'd get a good education, a safe job, smart friends. It probably sounds a lot like your father's list for you. We both had to face life alone to start with." He enjoyed the way Brisa's arms tightened around his waist. As if she would do what she could to make sure he didn't feel that way again. "But as a dad, I realized that what I had to do first was love Thea, and that was the easiest piece of the whole puzzle. It didn't have to make sense.

I'll listen to lectures about dark matter and swim coaches and spaceship engineering. No logic is required. Thea is Thea and I love her more than life. How in the world could I make a list of logical, reasonable characteristics and ever expect to experience the same kind of love? That makes no sense. I think that's what it takes to get through this life. A love that means more than logic."

"So you want a love that makes no sense?" Brisa asked, her lips pursed as she evaluated that.

"More than that, real love, the kind you and I want, it's beyond understanding, beyond plotting and planning. It finds us," he said.

"Are you kissing?" Thea asked in her loud stage whisper from the doorway to The Amazing Space Race Escape. "The Martian says she has to start our clock, or we'll run over into the next reservation."

Wade waved a hand. "One minute, Thea. We'll be right there."

She closed the door, but Wade knew her nose was still pressed against the glass. "Good. A ticking clock. Anyway, now I